The Mistletoe Inn

Center Point
Large Print

Also by Richard Paul Evans and available
from Center Point Large Print:

A Step of Faith
Walking on Water
The Mistletoe Promise

**This Large Print Book carries the
Seal of Approval of N.A.V.H.**

The Mistletoe Inn

RICHARD PAUL EVANS

CENTER POINT LARGE PRINT
THORNDIKE, MAINE

This Center Point Large Print edition is published in the year 2016 by arrangement with Simon & Schuster, Inc.

The text of this Large Print edition is unabridged.
In other aspects, this book may vary
from the original edition.
Printed in the United States of America
on permanent paper.
Set in 16-point Times New Roman type.

ISBN: 978-1-62899-917-4

Library of Congress Cataloging-in-Publication Data

Names: Evans, Richard Paul, author.
Title: The Mistletoe Inn / Richard Paul Evans.
Description: Center Point Large Print edition. | Thorndike, Maine : Center Point Large Print, 2016. | ©2015
Identifiers: LCCN 2015050714 | ISBN 9781628999174
        (hardcover : alk. paper)
Subjects: LCSH: Large type books. | Christmas stories. | GSAFD: Love stories.
Classification: LCC PS3555.V259 M56 2016 | DDC 813/.54—dc23
LC record available at http://lccn.loc.gov/2015050714

In memory of my mother
June Thorup Evans

Author's Note

A few years ago I decided to write a collection of holiday love stories: The Mistletoe Collection. The first book in that collection was 2014's bestselling *The Mistletoe Promise*. This book, *The Mistletoe Inn*, is the second. The third book (still unnamed, but it will have the word "Mistletoe" in the title) will come out in the fall of 2016. These books are not a trilogy; rather, they are three independent love stories abounding with inspiration, humor, and romance—a Christmas present for my readers.

That's not to say that there's *no* connection between the three books. In this novel, our protagonist, Kim Rossi (named after my third-grade teacher), is an aspiring romance writer working on a book titled *The Mistletoe Promise*. This is a bit of an inside joke. I used the title only for fun, as it has little to no bearing on the actual story or its outcome.

I hope you enjoy this holiday offering and that it fills your home and heart (and those of the people with whom you share this book) with joy, love, and peace.

Blessings,
Richard Paul Evans

Prologue

When I was eleven years old I was walking home from a friend's birthday party when I saw an ambulance parked in the driveway of my house. I dropped my party favors and sprinted home. When I got inside, the house was crowded with people: aunts and uncles, some neighbors, and our pastor. Everyone except my parents.

"What's going on?" I asked.

My aunt crouched down until we were eye level. "Kimmy, your mother tried to take her life."

The words froze my heart. "Is she still alive?"

"I don't know, honey. We're waiting to find out."

I began to cry, wiping my eyes on the sleeve of my blouse. "I need to see her."

"You shouldn't right now," my aunt said, gently taking me by my arms. I pulled free from her grasp and ran to my parents' room. A husky paramedic stopped me outside the bedroom door, grabbing me firmly by my waist. "Hold on there."

"Let go of me!" I shouted, struggling against his powerful grip.

"It's best that you not go in there."

"She's my mother!" I screamed.

"That's why it's best."

My father must have heard me. I stopped struggling when I saw him. He looked weary and in pain. He squatted down and put his arms around me. "She's going to be okay," he said. "Everything will be okay. I need you to wait out here while the paramedics finish up. We need to get Mom to the hospital, okay? We'll talk on the way there."

Someone, I don't remember who, took my hand and led me back to the front room and the somber faces. I could feel everyone's eyes on me. I felt like I was in one of those Tilt-A-Whirl rides at the carnival, the kind that spins you around until you don't know where you are. Or at least until you want to throw up.

Then the bedroom door opened and the room quieted as a processional emerged, a line of men carrying my mother out of the house on a stretcher, a blanket pulled up tightly to her neck, my father at her side, stoic and pale. I remember the heavy clomp of the paramedics' boots.

On the drive to the hospital I asked my dad, "Why did she try to kill herself?"

"Same as before," he said. "Sometimes it just takes her."

"Will she try again?"

He just looked ahead at the road. Even at that age, I knew that he was struggling to decide if he should tell me what I wanted to hear or the truth. "I don't know, sweetie. I hope not. But I don't know."

Twelve weeks later, on Christmas, my mother tried again. This time she didn't fail.

Chapter
One

The combined ballast of my life's abandonment is only balanced by the substantial weight of my father's love.

Kimberly Rossi's Diary

My mother attempted suicide four times before she finally succeeded. At least those are the attempts that I know about; there could have been more, as my father often ran interference, hiding things that he thought would hurt me. My mother suffered from major depression. She also had migraines. By most accounts they were unusually severe. She almost always had visual effects, seeing strange lines and flashes of light and sometimes hearing voices. When the migraines came she never left her room.

Doctors tried to help, though it seemed to me like they were bailing out a sinking boat with a paper cup. Most just medicated her with the latest trending mind drug: Valium, Xanax, Prozac, etc. A few told her to "buck up," which was like telling a stage-four cancer patient to just get over it. Then there were the insufferable people who said stupid things like, "I was depressed once. I went for a walk," or, "You have so much to be thankful for, how can you be depressed?" then smugly walked off as if they'd just performed a service to society.

With my mother almost always ill, my father did his best to pick up the slack. It was not unusual for him to come home from a long day of work, make dinner, clean the kitchen (with my help), then put in the laundry. I could never figure out why my father stayed with her.

The Christmas afternoon my mother died was the first time I ever saw my father cry. He also cried at her funeral, which for me was the most upsetting part of the day. I know that sounds weird, but in my young mind, my mother had died long before we buried her.

After the funeral, my aunt took me for a couple of days, until my father came and got me and we went on with our lives. Just like that. Just like nothing had happened.

My father, Robert Dante Rossi, didn't have a degree, but he was smart. He had started but never finished college (even though he insisted that I did). He was hardworking and good with people. I once heard one of his colleagues describe my father as "the kind of guy who could tell you to go to hell and you'd look forward to the trip."

He was a Vietnam vet and had served two years in the air cavalry, which meant he saw a lot of combat. He rarely talked about those experiences, but he didn't seem overly affected by them either, at least not in the way the movies like to paint Vietnam vets: handicapped in mind and spirit. I remember when I was fifteen I asked him if he had ever killed anyone. He was quiet for almost a minute, then looked at me and said, "I served my country."

When he got back from the war he went to

11

college for a year before deciding it wasn't for him. He took a job managing a Maverick convenience store in Henderson. After five years and as many promotions, he was in charge of the entire Las Vegas region for Maverick. I don't suppose that he ever made a lot of money, but I never felt like we were poor. My father was disciplined and frugal, the kind of guy who still mowed his own lawn and drove an old Ford Taurus.

He did his best to raise me alone. He got up early every day, made my lunch, then drove me to school. He took a late lunch break so he could pick me up after school. I usually just stayed with him as he finished his rounds, talking about my day, then doing my homework in the car when he went inside a store. He'd always return with a slushie drink, a chocolate MoonPie, and a couple of fashion or teen magazines—the previous months that they were about to throw out. I liked being with him.

When I was a little older he decided that as long as I was making the rounds with him I should get paid for it, and he hired me as an employee. I would go into the stores he was visiting and wipe down the soda dispensers and clean the glass on the refrigerators. That's pretty much how my life went during my teenage years.

My memories of my mother were vague and hazy, perhaps because they were so heavily wrapped in trauma. Most of them were of her in a dark room lying in bed. I didn't really know her. I suppose my father could have filled in the blanks, but the truth is, I didn't want them filled in. The few times my father started to tell me about her I stopped him. "I don't want to know," I said. Looking back, I think that hurt him, but my intent was the opposite. I was trying to prove to him that I was okay without her. I felt my mother was a failure and a traitor, not just to me but even more to my father. I deserved someone who cared enough about me to stick around and so did he. We both deserved someone better than her.

At least that's how I saw it.

In high school I was one of those girls who always had to have a boyfriend. Starting in the eighth grade, I had a string of boyfriends until my senior year in high school when I started dating Kent Clark. (Yes, people teased him about his name. His friends called him "Steel of Man.") Kent was a popular guy. He was on the high school basketball team and lettered in track and wrestling as well.

Two years after high school, Kent proposed to me and I said yes. My dad, with a neighbor woman's help, went through all the work of reserving the reception center, caterer, flowers—the whole matrimonial shebang.

Then the Steel of Man kryptonited the day of

the wedding, running off with a high school girlfriend he'd dated before me. It was the most humiliating experience of my life. Not the worst experience. Just the most humiliating.

Alone, I continued on with college, pursuing my general education where my father had dropped out—the University of Nevada–Las Vegas. That's where I met Danny, another basketball player. Two years later, I was a fiancée again.

Danny was a walk-on for UNLV's basketball team and quickly moved up to starting forward. I should have known that the odds were against any kind of real relationship with a rising basketball star, but I thought I was in love and was caught up in the thrill of being the future wife of a professional athlete. I soon learned exactly what that meant, which was, to Danny, almost nothing. The more he rose in the public's (and his own) view, the less he regarded *us*. I began hearing that he was not behaving like a betrothed man on road trips. The next year he was drafted by the Orlando Magic and left Vegas, and me, behind.

Twice burned by young athletes, I found Marcus, who was nine years older than me. I also met him at college. He was my history professor, which should have been my first red flag.

My father wasn't thrilled with any of the guys I'd been with, but for the most part kept his silence. For Marcus he made an exception. He said that a professor dating his student was as unethical as a psychiatrist courting a patient. Still, as much as it pained him, he believed in letting me make my choices no matter how stupid they were. I thought it a great accomplishment that Marcus didn't leave me before we reached the altar.

In retrospect, I wish he had. I learned on our honeymoon night the extent of his cruelty. He got drunk at our wedding—drunk enough that I drove to our hotel while he yelled at me about how the wedding had been all about me, how I had neglected him, and how selfish I was. In the pain of the moment I begged his forgiveness, but he still made me sleep on the couch in the guest section of the suite my father had paid for. That was our honeymoon night. I suppose it was a preview of how my life would be with him. Before we were married, Marcus couldn't keep his hands off me. Now he wouldn't touch me. I was embarrassed to undress in front of him since he started calling me chunky and telling me that I needed to lose weight, even though I knew I didn't. He criticized me constantly, not just the way I looked, but the things I said, the things I thought, even the music I liked. He constantly called me stupid or ditzy. Nothing I did met his expectations.

What I didn't realize until later, much later, was that emotional manipulation was his modus operandi. He was a master at it. He should have taught psychology instead of history. He controlled our relationship by keeping me emotionally needy, giving me just enough "love" to not give up, but never enough to feel satisfied. It was like filling a dog's water bowl half-full. I never felt like I was enough, and apparently I wasn't. I should have left him, but I didn't. I suppose that I believed, like my father must have, that marriage was for better or for worse.

Three years after our marriage, Marcus was offered a bigger paycheck at the University of Colorado in Boulder. I hated leaving my father and Las Vegas, but it was a promotion and Marcus was insistent. I didn't fight it. I believed that supporting my husband was the right thing to do. Also, Marcus frequently complained that I was too close to my father and that it got in the way of our marriage. I thought that the experience of being alone in a strange town would bring us closer together. It didn't.

I filed for divorce two years later when Marcus was exposed in a campus investigation for ethical misconduct, something you may have read about in the *Huffington Post*. I'll never forget the night he told me. In a cruel twist of irony, it was Valentine's Day and I had spent the day making him a romantic candlelit dinner. When I stopped crying I asked, "Why did you cheat on me?"

"You're too clingy," he said stoically. "You were suffocating me. You forced me into it."

"I forced you to cheat on me?" I said.

"Yes, you did," he said. "Besides, monogamy is unnatural. Anyone with half a brain knows that."

That evening when I called my father and told him what had happened, he never once said "I told you so." He just wanted to beat Marcus to a pulp, and likely would have if he'd been there.

The next day the press arrived at our apartment. You wouldn't believe the things they asked me.

Press: How do you feel about your husband being sexually involved with six university students?

Me: You're really asking me that?

Press: Are you upset?

Me: . . .

After our separation, Marcus ran off with not one but *two* of his female students. Alone again, I moved forty miles south to Denver. My father wanted me to come back to Las Vegas, but shame kept me away. I didn't want to return home a failure, even if that's what I was.

I got a job in Thornton, a suburb of Denver, as a finance officer at a Lexus car dealership, which is where I was the winter this story began.

As I look back at where I was in my life at that time, it wasn't so much that my life wasn't what I *thought* it would be, as that's likely true of all of us. Rather, it's that it wasn't what I wanted it to be. I wanted someone to build a life with, someone who would think about me when they weren't with me. I wanted someone who loved me.

I also wanted to live a life of consequence. I wanted to be someone who mattered, which leads to something else you should know about me. In spite of my catastrophic love life, more than anything I wanted to be a romance writer. I know that sounds strange. Me writing about romance is like a vegan writing about barbecue. Still, I couldn't let the dream go. So when I got a flyer in the mail for a romance writers' retreat at the Mistletoe Inn, a little voice inside told me that it might be my last chance to find what I was looking for. That voice was far more right than I could have imagined—just not in the way I ever imagined it would be.

Chapter

Two

They say love is blind, but it's not. Infatuation is blind. Emotional neediness is blind. Love sees the fault—it just sees beyond it as well.

Kimberly Rossi's Diary

Denver was cold. Like arctic cold. It was a late Friday afternoon in November when Rachelle, the other finance manager, came to my office. Rachelle was gorgeous. Before being hired at Lexus she had been a Denver Broncos cheerleader, which also made her the finance manager with whom our male buyers most wanted to process their car purchases. Invariably they flirted with her, which she used to her advantage. She sold more paint protectant than the rest of us. If she wasn't so picky about men, she would have broken up half the marriages in Denver.

"Hey, Kim," she said, leaning through my door. "Could you please take this last customer? I've got an early date tonight with a guy as hot as a solar flare."

"You say that about every guy you date," I said.

"I can't help it if I'm a heat magnet. And you might like this one."

I shook my head. "Go on your date."

"You're a doll," she said, mincing away.

"You're a Barbie doll," I said under my breath.

The man Rachelle had passed on to me was in his late fifties and, in spite of it being winter, wore plaid golf pants, a lemon-yellow sweater, and a pink Polo golf shirt that stretched over his ample belly. He also wore a beret, which failed to cover his bald spot. His forehead was beaded with sweat that he constantly wiped with the handkerchief he carried. I couldn't believe that Rachelle thought this guy was my speed. No, actually I could. She had always treated me as a wallflower.

The man sat down in one of the vinyl chairs in front of my desk while Bart, the salesman who had sold the car, introduced us.

"Kim, this is Mr. Craig, the proud owner of a new GX 460." He turned back to his huffing client. "Kimberly is one of our finance officers. She'll take good care of you."

"I do hope so," the man said in a thin, whiny voice.

"I'll run to service and make sure they've got your car ready to drive home," Bart said to the man, then left my office.

"It's a pleasure to meet you, Mr. Craig," I said. "I'll get your information typed up and get you out of here to enjoy your new vehicle."

I was entering the purchase information when the man suddenly blurted out, "Is it hot in here or is it just . . . *you?*"

I looked up at him. He was gazing at me with an insipid grin.

"It's a little warm," I said. "If you like I can turn down the heat."

"No," he said, a little thrown that I hadn't fallen for his line. "I like it hot." Then he started to hum that song, ". . . *some like it hot, some sweat when the heat is on . . .*" He was definitely sweating.

"Okay," I said. "What's your phone number?"

"My phone number," he repeated. "My phone number." He pretended to look through his pockets. Then he said, "I seem to have misplaced it. Can I have yours?"

"Excuse me?" I said.

He just looked at me.

"Your phone number?" I repeated.

"It's 555-445-3989."

I typed in the number. I hoped that the awkwardness had successfully dissuaded him but it hadn't. A few minutes later he said, "Your name is Kimberly?"

"Yes."

"May I call you Kim?"

"Yes, you may," I said, continuing typing.

A beat later he asked, "What time?"

I looked up. "What time . . . what?"

"What time may I call you, Kim?"

I breathed out slowly. "Okay, Mr. Craig . . ."

"Tim."

"I'm flattered, Tim, but I'm not in the market right now, so you just hang on to those gems for some other lucky gal."

He slightly blushed. "Sorry."

"No need to be sorry," I said. "Now, if you'll just fill out your insurance information."

He silently filled out the paperwork. When he finished he said, "Are you almost off work?"

I looked up from my computer.

"Because, if you are, I'll take you for a ride in my new car. Maybe we could go to dinner. Or *something*."

"Just a minute," I said, standing. "May I get you some water?"

"I'm not thirsty."

"I meant to cool you off."

"No, I'm good," he said.

"All right, I'll be right back."

I walked into the employee break room and grabbed myself a ginger ale. My manager, Steve, was sitting at a table working on his iPad. Steve was a good guy, and one of my few real friends at the dealership.

"Just kill me now," I said. "Please."

"What's going on?"

"Mr. Beret is. He thinks the car should come with a dealer-installed woman."

"That would increase sales," Steve said. "I wonder if it's ever been done."

"You're not being helpful."

"Sorry. Is it the GX?"

"Yes."

"Wasn't that Rachelle's?"

"Was. She asked me to take it for her. She had a hot date."

"Rachelle always has a hot date," he said. "Want me to finish up for you?"

"No. I just needed someone to commiserate with."

"Consider yourself co-commiserated."

"Thanks."

I started to walk back to my office when Steve said, "Just tell him you're not interested in dating."

"Yeah, I did."

"It didn't help?"

"No."

As I walked back to my office I thought, *Is that what everyone thinks about me?*

Chapter
Three

*There have been seasons of my life
when rejection rained down.
And then there have been typhoons.*

Kimberly Rossi's Diary

In spite of the Denver traffic, my commute wasn't too bad. I was glad to get home. For once I had plans for the evening. I had a second date with Collin, a man I had met at the dealership. He wasn't buying a car—he was a vendor who sold tools to our service bay. I had gone to get a bottle of water from the waiting area and he was there drinking a coffee. He struck up a conversation by the coffeemaker, then asked me out.

I stopped by the Java Hut for a coffee, then headed home. I lived in a decent but inexpensive apartment complex in Thornton, about a half hour from the dealership. Walking into my apartment with my hands filled with my coffee, purse, and mail, I heard my phone chirp with a text message.

"You will have to wait," I said to myself. I unlocked my door and went inside. I set down my coffee and mail, then dug through my purse for my phone. I lifted it to read the text message. It was from Collin.

Sorry. Something came up. Rain check? I'll call you.

I'm sure you will, I thought. I sighed. I liked the guy. I felt like a rejection magnet.

I started looking through my mail. There was a letter from the Boulder County Clerk's office. I tore it open.

IN THE DISTRICT COURT OF THE BOULDER JUDICIAL DISTRICT OF THE STATE OF COLORADO, IN AND FOR THE COUNTY OF BOULDER

Kimberly Rossi,
Plaintiff,
vs.
Marcus Y. Stewart,
Defendant.
Case No.: 4453989
DECREE OF DIVORCE

This matter came before the court on the seventh day of October 2012. It appears from the records and files of this action that a Complaint was filed and served upon the Defendant.

The rest of the letter was just typical legal jargon, which basically said over and over that we were over. However, the last line stopped me.

3. Name Change. Wife will retain the last name of Rossi.

Rossi again, I thought. *Back to where I started.* The paper was dated and signed by the magistrate and judge. The formalities of our divorce had taken longer than I had expected, as Marcus had fought the divorce the whole way. He wasn't trying to keep me, he was trying to keep his money.

I don't know why the letter made our separation feel any more official—I hadn't seen Marcus for more than six months—but it did. He was a liar, a cheater, and he didn't love me. So why was I so sad?

I flipped through the rest of the mail. As a child, I had thought mail was something magical. There were handwritten letters, cards, and thank-you notes. Now it seemed to be nothing but circulars and junk mail—the physical equivalent of spam.

Then I saw a letter from a publisher.

"Please, please, please." I tore open the envelope.

Monday, October 12, 2012

Dear Author,

They didn't use my name. Not a good sign.

Thank you for giving us the opportunity to consider your manuscript. We read it with interest. While there was much to like about your book, we regret we will not be making an offer of publication. We do not feel that we are the right publishing house to success-fully publish your book.

Thank you for thinking of us, and we wish you every success in finding a publisher for your work.

Yours sincerely,
Sharlene Drexell

Strike three. I sighed loudly. Actually, it was more of a groan. The universe must have con-spired to bring me so much rejection at once. I was almost in a daze as I looked through the rest of the mail, which I did more out of habit than of interest.

That's when I saw the card for a writers' conference at the Mistletoe Inn.

Chapter

Four

There are people whom we've never met in person yet feel closer to than those we brush up against in real life.

Kimberly Rossi's Diary

I must be on a wannabe-writer list somewhere. Six years ago I attended a two-day writing seminar in San Francisco and ever since then I've gotten notices every month about the latest writing conference, seminar, retreat, or authors' workshop—a faucet I'd probably turn off if I had any idea where the spigot was. But this one looked interesting.

THE MISTLETOE INN
WRITERS' RETREAT

Attention Aspiring Romance Writers–

Bring Your Brand of Love to the Mistletoe Inn!
This Holiday Give Yourself a Once-in-a-Lifetime
Christmas Gift.
Writing Workshops • Panel Discussions
Agent Pitch Sessions • Open Mic Readings

Special Keynote Speaker

H. T. Cowell

December 10–17, 2012
$2,199 includes room /
breakfast & lunch each day

What especially caught my eye was the name H. T. Cowell—and not just because his name was printed in type twice the size of everything else on the piece. Cowell had earned twenty-point type. You probably remember him, or at least his name. He was once the bestselling romance writer in America.

Actually he was one of the bestselling writers of any genre. He didn't just dominate the genre, he defined it. What Stephen King did for horror, Cowell did for romance. He's also the writer who made *me* want to be a writer. For years I read everything he wrote. And then, like the other men in my life, he was gone. The difference was, no one knew where he went.

Cowell, who was reclusive to begin with—his books didn't even have an author photo—was one of those literary-world enigmas like J. D. Salinger or E. M. Forster who, at the top of their game, disappeared into the shadowy ether of obscurity, like a literary version of Amelia Earhart.

Of course, that just made him more intriguing to his readers. The year he stopped writing was the same year Danny left me. I think, on some level, I had fallen in love with H. T. Cowell. Or at least the idea of him. I couldn't believe that after all this time he was coming out in public.

I looked over the advertisement, then set it apart from the rest of the mail. The event was pricey, at least for me, but it was, as advertised, a once-in-a-lifetime experience. And right now I needed a once-in-a-lifetime experience. I needed something to look forward to. Frankly, I needed something to live for. I looked over the advertisement again.

To book your space, call 555-2127.
Or register online.

I made myself some ramen noodles for dinner, then was turning on *The Bachelor* when my phone rang. It was my father.

"Hey, Dad."

"*Ciao, bella.* How are you?"

"I'm okay," I said. "How are you?"

"*Bene, bene.*" He sounded tired. "I wanted to make sure you're still coming out for Thanksgiving."

"Of course."

"And Christmas?"

"That too."

"Do you know what day you'll be here?"

"For Thanksgiving, Wednesday afternoon. I'm not sure about Christmas. What day is Christmas this year?"

"It's on a Tuesday."

"I'll probably be out the Sunday before, if that's okay."

"Great, but you might have to take a cab from

the airport. There's a chance I might not be back until late Sunday night."

"Where are you going?"

"A group of us are taking a Harley ride over to Albuquerque."

"That sounds fun. Just be careful."

"I always am."

"You know, your Harley has two seats."

"Are you inviting yourself?"

"I meant you might want to take a friend. A female friend."

"Well, don't faint, but I've invited someone. I'm waiting for her to get back to me."

This was a first. "Does this *someone* have a name?"

"Alice. She works down at the VA. We've been spending some time together lately."

"It's about time."

"It's nothing serious," he quickly added. "I'm not really looking for anything but a little companionship."

"That's a good place to start."

"How about you?" he asked. "Any new friends?"

"Nothing special."

"No need to rush into anything. And I'm so glad you're coming out. We'll have a wonderful, relaxing time."

"That sounds nice," I said. "Nothing like the dry desert heat to warm your bones. Especially at Christmas."

"Which reminds me. What do you want for Christmas?"

"I don't need anything," I said.

"I didn't ask what you needed, I asked what you wanted. Besides, I'm just spending your inheritance anyway. You want it now or after I check out and taxes are higher?"

"I'd rather you not talk about 'checking out.' You're going to live forever."

"Ah, denial." He was quiet a moment, then said softly, "We all check out sometime, baby."

"Can we please not talk about this?"

"Sorry. So help me out here. What can I give you for Christmas? My mutual funds did well this year. I'd like to do something meaningful."

I hesitated a moment, then said, "Well, there is something."

"Name it."

"I wouldn't ask for you to do the whole thing, but maybe you could help me with part of it. There's a romance writers' conference in Vermont that I'd like to go to."

"Still holding on to the dream?"

"Barely," I said.

"I'm glad you are," he said. "You're such a talented writer. You hang on to it. Without dreams, life is a desert."

"With a love life like mine I should be writing horror, not romance."

"We're Italians. We invented the word *romance.*

So you just hang on to that dream until it happens. That's what gets us up in the morning."

I sighed. "So what do you dream about?"

"My daughter," he said without hesitation. "Mostly. And her next visit. I can't wait to see you."

"I can't wait to see you, Dad. I love you."

"I love you too, girl."

Chapter
Five

*Like a balloon, a full heart
is easier to puncture.*

Kimberly Rossi's Diary

The next few weeks passed slowly. We had several major snowstorms, and business at the dealership was slow. There's a predictable psychology of car sales and people don't like to buy new cars in the snow, unless, of course, there's too much snow and they suddenly need a four-wheel-drive vehicle.

I was very glad for Thanksgiving break. I left work early Wednesday afternoon and drove myself out to the airport for my flight to Vegas.

Much can be said about the Denver airport, and much is. There are groups of conspiracy theorists who believe that the Denver airport is the secret headquarters of the Illuminati, New World Order, or the Neo-Nazi party, evidenced by the fact that from the air, the airport purportedly looks like a giant swastika.

My favorite theory is that the airport is an underground base for aliens. However, if the airport *were* run by aliens, you would think they would do a better job of managing things. A technically advanced civilization that can traveL at light speed should, for instance, be able to get your luggage to you.

And then there's *Blucifer*, the airport's famous

thirty-two-foot, anatomically correct blue horse sculpture. With its blazing red-bulb eyes and crazed expression, the piece is enough to stir fear in the most seasoned flier. What adds to the sculpture's lore is the fact that in a Frankenstein's-monster sort of way, the creation killed its creator. Luis Jiménez, the sculpture's artist, was crushed when a piece of the massive sculpture fell on him.

Not surprisingly, the airport was slammed with pre-Thanksgiving traffic, and the security line at Denver International looked more like the start of the Boston Marathon than any sort of a civilized queue. The insanity didn't ease after the security checkpoint, as every gate was thronged with travelers.

As I was at the gate checking on a possible seat upgrade, a harried young father walked up next to me.

"There's been a mistake," he said to a ticket agent, laying a stack of boarding passes on the counter in front of him. "They've scattered our seats throughout the plane."

The agent, who looked as if he'd had better days, glanced down at the passes, then back up. "I'm sorry," he said gruffly, "the flight's over-booked. There's nothing I can do about it now."

"But we have four children," he said. "Three of them are under four. Our flight's already been delayed three hours. These kids are going crazy."

"You should have thought of that when you booked the tickets."

"I should have thought that you would delay the flight three hours?" the man asked.

"A delayed flight's always a possibility, sir. But I meant you should have booked your seats together."

"They were all booked at the same time six weeks in advance. There was no reason to believe that you would scatter them."

"*I* didn't do anything to your seats," he said defensively. "And it's out of my hands. There's nothing I can do about it."

I looked sympathetically at the frustrated man, wondering what he would do.

"Can I talk to a manager?" he asked, doing his best to remain civil.

"She's not here right now," the agent said. "We're a bit busy." He scooped up the passes and handed them back. "I'll call you up to the counter when she can talk. But, like I said, the flight's overbooked. I doubt there's anything she can do."

The man took his passes and returned to a seat next to his wife, who looked equally stressed— more so after he relayed the information he'd just received.

I was told that all the first-class passengers had checked in, so I took a seat directly across from the man and his family. I watched the exhausted couple become increasingly exasperated as their small children grew more impatient. About forty-five minutes later the man still hadn't been called up so he returned to the counter. The agent spoke loud enough that I could hear him say curtly, "I told you I'd call you up when she had time."

The man again returned to his seat. Busy or not, there was no excuse for the agent's rudeness, I thought.

Another half hour passed when the man stood and walked back up to the counter. The gate agent stiffened as the man approached and I expected an explosive confrontation. Instead, the man said, "Hey, about my request. Don't worry about it."

The agent looked at him with a blank expression. "What?"

"It's cool, really. You're busy, don't worry about it. We're good."

The agent looked even more disturbed than before. "What?"

"Look," the man said calmly. "After four hours in this airport with these kids, we're exhausted. If you're offering free babysitting, we're all over that. They can be someone else's problems." He turned and walked back to his seat, leaving the agent speechless. Less than ten minutes later the agent paged the man over the intercom, then said nothing as he handed the man a pile of boarding passes, presumably all next to each other.

Well played, I thought. *Well played.*

• • •

My flight landed in Vegas at around five. Not surprisingly the Las Vegas airport was even more slammed than Denver's. I retrieved my bag from the carousel, then called my father. "I'm here."

"I'm just parked in the cell phone lot," he said. "I'll be right there."

Just a few minutes after I arrived at the curb my father pulled up in his metallic-blue 2004 Ford Taurus. He climbed out to hug me. One of the effects of not seeing my father for such long stretches of time was that he always looked older. But this time he was thinner too. Regardless, it was always good to see him. We embraced and he kissed my face all over until I laughed—just as he had done when I was a little girl.

"It's so good to see you, sweetie."

"It's good to see you, Dad. You lost weight."

"It happens," he said.

"I wish it would happen to me."

"You don't need to lose weight. You look perfect." He grabbed my bag and threw it into the backseat of his car. "Are you hungry?"

"Famished."

"Good. I thought we'd stop by Salvatore's on the way home." When we were on the freeway he asked, "How was your flight?"

"Crowded," I said. "People were grumpy."

"Crowds make people grumpy," he said.

"Nothing like holiday travel to foul some people's mood."

"Not you," I said.

He smiled. "No, not me. I get to see my girl."

We stopped at my father's favorite Italian restaurant, Cucina Salvatore. I hadn't been there for years, not since I'd moved to Colorado. The owner, Salvatore, loudly greeted my father as we walked in.

"Roberto, *bello*. It has been too long."

"You say that every time," my father said. "I was here just last week."

"You are *famiglia*. It is always too long. *Sempre troppo tempo*."

"He says that to everyone," my father said to me.

Salvatore gestured toward me. "How is it you are always with beautiful women?"

"Oh really?" I said.

"This is my daughter," my father said.

"*Questa bella donna è la tua figlia? No!*" Salvatore put his hands on my cheeks and kissed me. "They grow too fast."

Salvatore sat us at a small table near the corner of the restaurant. "For family, the best table in the house," he said. "*Buon appetito*."

After he had left, my father smiled, then said, "Always the best table in the house." Then he told me that Salvatore had said that about two other tables.

We ordered bruschetta with baked garlic, sun-dried tomatoes, and goat cheese for an appetizer, then shared a Caprese salad. For our *primi piatti* I ordered a scallop risotto and my father ordered the mushroom gnocchi. For our second plate my father ordered Florentine steak while I had breaded chicken cacciatore.

After we'd been served our meals, my father asked, "So how's work?"

"Living the dream," I said sarcastically.

He nodded understandingly. He took a bite of steak, then said, "Tell me about this writers' conference."

"It's small. Intimate. From what I read, it's more than just a conference, it's a weeklong retreat with daily workshops where I can refine my book. And there will be real agents I can show my book to. But the best part is that my favorite writer of all time is going to be there. H. T. Cowell."

"I don't think I know who that is," my father said. "What has he written?"

"Nothing you would have read. He's a romance writer."

"Did Mom read him?" he asked. "She loved those romance books."

The question bothered me. "No. He came after her."

I think he sensed how uncomfortable I was and changed the subject. "Have you ever shown your book to an agent before?"

"No. I've sent it to a few publishers, but they just sent back rejection letters." I took a drink of wine. "Maybe it's just not good enough. Maybe I'm not good enough."

"Stop that," my father said. "All great artists get rejections. It's part of what defines them. Decca Records turned down the Beatles."

"I'm not the Beatles," I said. "And I'm no great artist."

"Why? Because you know yourself? A prophet is without honor in his own country, but more so in his own mind."

"I'm not a prophet either."

"But you might be a great writer," he said. "Or will be." My dad leaned forward. "Writing and work aside, how are you doing? How are you handling the divorce?"

"I'm fine," I said. "I'm doing really well."

For a moment he looked deep into my eyes, then said, "Remember when you were a teenager and you told me that you hadn't taken my Buick with your friends?"

I wasn't sure why he chose this moment to bring up that not-so-pleasant memory. "Yes."

"Well, you're no better a liar now than you were then."

My eyes filled with tears. Then I bowed my head and began to cry. My father reached across the table and took my hand. "I'm sorry."

I wiped my eyes with my napkin, then looked

back at him. "Why doesn't anybody want me? What's wrong with me?"

My father looked anguished. "Honey, there's nothing wrong with you."

I continued wiping my eyes. "You haven't really liked any of the guys I dated."

"I liked that Briton guy. The med student."

"That lasted only four weeks," I said. "I saw him on Facebook. He's married now, has two children and his own practice. He's doing well."

The moment fell into silence. Our waiter, Mario, came over and refilled our water glasses from a carafe. After he left I said, "You didn't like Marcus."

"No," he said, failing to hide the anger that Marcus's name still provoked. "He was a five-star loser. I saw that train wreck a mile off."

I shook my head slowly. "Why didn't I?"

He looked at me for a long time, then said, "Maybe when you figure that out, you won't be lonely."

I frowned. "Maybe." We both went back to eating. After a few minutes I said, "Well, at least I have you."

My father stopped eating, then looked at me thoughtfully. "That brings up something," he said slowly. His forehead furrowed. "You know when we were on the phone and you said I was going to live forever?" I just looked at him. He looked uncomfortable. "Three weeks ago I had a colonoscopy. They, uh . . ." He hesitated, looking into my fearful eyes. "They found a tumor."

I set down my fork. "But it's benign . . . ?"

He let out a nearly inaudible groan. "I have colon cancer."

I couldn't speak.

"Unfortunately, we didn't catch it early, so it's regionalized. It's what they call stage 3A."

Tears began to well up in my eyes. "I can't believe this."

"Now hold on, it's not as bad as it sounds. I know, stage three sounds like I've already got a foot in the grave, but I don't. There's an almost seventy percent survival rate. I'll take those odds any day of the week. Heck, just taking my Harley out on the road I have worse odds."

"Where are you getting care?"

"At the VA."

"The veterans hospital? You might as well just hang yourself."

"You're being dramatic. It's not that way."

I broke down crying. He took my hand. When I could speak, I said, "Can we go home now?"

He leaned over the table and kissed my forehead, then said, "Whatever you want, sweetheart. Whatever you want."

Chapter

Six

*How different life would be if we knew
just how little of it we actually possessed.*

Kimberly Rossi's Diary

My father's house was simple but beautiful—a typical Las Vegas rambler with a rock-and-white-stucco exterior surrounded by palm trees. It wasn't a large home, and everything was on one floor—three bedrooms, two baths—but there was plenty of room for the two of us.

In spite of my aching heart, or perhaps because of it, I was especially glad to be back. After all this time it still felt like home.

My father gave me his keys to the house, then grabbed my suitcase and followed me in. In the foyer was a large new saltwater fish aquarium filled with beautiful exotic fish, his newest hobby.

"How are your fish?" I asked.

"The fish," he said, sounding a little exasperated. "I had an incident last week. I purchased one of those triggerfish. It started eating the other fish, including my hundred-dollar pygmy angel-fish."

"Expensive hobby," I said.

"Too expensive for my budget," he said. "Never should have done it."

He carried my bag to my old bedroom and set it down next to the bed. "I washed the sheets and everything."

"Thanks, Dad." There was an uneasy awkwardness between us, as if he wasn't sure if he should leave me alone or not. Finally I asked, "Are you ready for tomorrow?"

"Just about. I baked the pies this morning."

"*You* baked pies?"

"It's something new I'm trying," he said. "I got the recipes off the Internet. And I had a little help. That woman I told you about from the VA hospital. She came over and helped me cook."

"You mean Alice?" I said.

He grinned. "Alice. As in, Alice's Restaurant."

"Whatever that is," I said.

"So I made a pumpkin pie and a pecan pie. The pecan pie was a little tricky, but it turned out all right."

"I'm glad that she came over," I said. "I don't like you being alone all the time."

"I'm not alone. I've got fish."

"If they don't all eat each other."

I suspect that he guessed I was just making small talk to avoid the cancerous elephant in the room, because he sat down on my bed next to me and put his arm around me. "Let me tell you something. When I was in Nam, there was this guy I served with named Gordie Ewell. He was regular infantry, served four years in combat. That man was indestructible. He was in some of the most intense battles of the war: Hamburger Hill, Khe Sanh, and Cu Chi. He survived a crash in a downed helicopter, had a jeep blown up beneath him from a land mine, was hit by grenade shrapnel in a trench, got bit by a viper and shot twice. But nothing stopped him. The men nicknamed him Boomerang because he always came back.

"When he was finally released, he was awarded three Purple Hearts. He went home to Brooklyn in June of seventy-three, around the time the war started winding down.

"About a month later he went in to get a wisdom tooth pulled. He was given too much anesthetic and died in the dentist chair."

I just looked at my father. "Exactly what part of that was supposed to make me feel better?"

"I'm just saying that when it's your time, it's your time. I know that might sound foreboding, but I take hope in it." He put his hands on my cheeks. "I don't believe it's my time, girl. We've still got plenty of good years ahead of us, you and I." He kissed me on the forehead, then stood. "Now go to bed. We've got a lot to do tomorrow."

"Good night, Dad."

"Good night, sweetheart." He walked to the door, then looked back. "Our best years are still to come. Don't forget that."

"I hope you're right," I said.

"I know I'm right," he said, thumping his fist against his heart. "I know it." He walked out, shutting the door behind him.

I undressed, turned out the light, then crawled under the covers. I cried myself to sleep.

Chapter
Seven

Sometimes the most whole people are those who come from the most broken circumstances.

Kimberly Rossi's Diary

Not surprisingly, I didn't sleep well. Thoughts of my father's cancer played through my mind like a bad song you can't get rid of. I sat bolt upright in the middle of the night after dreaming that I was at his funeral.

In spite of my lack of sleep, I got up early enough to go outside and watch the sun rise over the River Mountains. It was cool outside, probably in the low sixties, but practically sweltering compared to the freeze I'd left back in Denver.

I put on my walking shoes, sweatpants, and a Denver Broncos sweatshirt and walked about six miles, trying to clear my head a little before going back to the house. I was hoping that the walk would make me feel better, but it only made my mind focus more on my father's cancer. I started crying twice, once when I was almost home, so I just kept walking for another mile. I didn't want my dad to see me crying—not that I could have hidden it anymore, as my eyes were already red and puffy. When I walked into the house my father was in the kitchen making breakfast.

"I made you some oatmeal." My father said nothing about my puffy eyes, which I was grateful for. He hugged me, then handed me a bowl. "I made it just the way you like it, with cream, walnuts, raisins, and a lot of brown sugar. Too much brown sugar."

"Thanks, Dad." I sat down to eat.

"How was your walk?"

"It was okay," I said.

My father poured cream over his oatmeal, then sat down across from me. "How did you sleep?"

"It's just good to be back home," I said, ignoring his question.

"It's always good when you're home," he replied. "You don't have to live in Colorado."

"I know," I said.

After we finished eating, my father, as tradition dictated, put on the Carpenters' Christmas album and Karen's rich voice filled our home.

We had a lot of cooking to do, which I was glad for. I needed something to occupy my mind. My tasks were pecan-crusted sweet potato casserole and corn bread stuffing.

I noticed that my father set the table with two extra settings.

"Are we having guests?"

"I invited a couple of men from the hospital. Chuck and Joel. They don't have any family around. Is that all right?"

"Of course. What about Alice?"

"She's in Utah with her children. Her son owns an Internet company up there."

Neither of us spoke for a while. The emotion returned and I purposely kept turned away from my father, occasionally dabbing my cheeks with a napkin or dish towel. I was chopping pecans for the casserole when he walked up beside me. "What's wrong?"

I kept chopping, avoiding eye contact. "You mean, besides you dying?"

He put his hand on mine to stop me. "I told you I'm not dying."

"Relying on care from the veterans hospital is not exactly filling me with confidence. Las Vegas has one of the best cancer facilities in America. Why don't you go there?"

"Why should I get any better treatment than anyone else?"

"What you should get is the best treatment available."

"I am. The VA is what's available. I can't afford any fancy cancer center."

"But your insurance . . ."

"My Medicare covers the VA."

I shook my head. "There's got to be another way to pay for it."

He didn't say anything.

After a moment I said, "Do you know what makes this even worse, if that were possible? It's that this is happening on Thanksgiving. Now I've lost another holiday since Mom obliterated Christmas and Marcus destroyed Valentine's Day.

Now I just need some tragedy on Halloween and Easter."

"I'm sorry," he said. "I shouldn't have told you."

"Of course you should have told me."

"Then you have to believe me that everything is going to be all right."

"What does that even mean? *All right*. Like, dying is *all right?*"

He was quiet a moment, then said, "If it comes to that."

"If it comes to that? Why do you have to be so okay about your death?"

"Why do you have to be so *un*okay about it? Everyone dies."

I looked at him, fighting back tears. "Not you."

"Why not me?"

"Because you're all I have." I broke down crying. "You're all I've ever had."

He put his arms around me and held me close, rubbing his fingers through my hair. Then he said, "You're right. That's not fair of me, is it? You're all I have too."

I sobbed in his arms for several minutes. After I quieted he said, "I meant it when I said I don't think it's my time. But if, God forbid, it is, remember that death is the punctuation at the end of the sentence. It's up to us to decide what kind of punctuation it will be—a period or an exclamation point."

"Or a question mark."

"Sometimes that too," he said. "But if this is the end, and I don't think it is, do we want to leave our sentence unfinished? Or do we make it the best ending possible?" I didn't answer and he leaned forward. "What should we do?"

"We make it the best ending possible."

He smiled. "Good girl. Now have a little faith that things will work out all right. Besides, we have a lot to be thankful for."

At the moment I couldn't think of a single thing. "Like what?"

"Like this moment," he said. "Right now."

As I wiped the tears from my eyes the timer on the oven went off.

"There's the rolls," he said. "And I know you're grateful for those." He donned oven mitts, then opened the oven door. "Just about there." My father made the best Parker House rolls on the planet. He brushed butter on top of the rolls, then shut the oven again.

"How's everything coming on your end?" he asked.

"It's getting there."

"Good. Our friends will be here in a half hour."

My father was carving the turkey with an electric knife when the doorbell rang. "That must be Chuck and Joel. You mind getting that?"

"No problem." I walked to the front door and opened it. The men standing in the doorway didn't look like I thought they would, as I was expecting two of my father's Vietnam buddies. They weren't. One was much older than my father. He was short and had an exaggerated potbelly. He was also blind, which I could tell because his eyes were milky white. The other man was closer to my age, maybe a few years younger. He was cute with thick, curly black hair and the rugged square jaw of a marine. He leaned on a crutch as he was missing his right leg and left forearm.

"Happy Thanksgiving," I said. "Please come in."

"Thanks, ma'am," the younger man said.

"Gentlemen," my father shouted from the kitchen. "Come on in."

"You must be mistaken," the old man said, laughing. "There's no gentlemen here."

My father walked out of the kitchen to greet them. "Sorry, just carving the bird. Come in, come in."

The older man held on to the stump of the younger man's arm as they walked into the house.

"It smells like heaven," the older man said.

"You're not going to leave hungry," I said.

"Who is this lovely young woman answering your door?" the old man asked.

"And all this time I thought you were blind," my father said.

"I can't see," he said. "But I'm not blind." He turned toward me. "I'm Chuck, young lady." He reached out and I gave him my hand. He took it and kissed it. "Thank you for letting an old man crash your party."

"It's our pleasure," I said.

"I'm Joel," the other man said, extending his hand. "I really appreciate the invitation. I'm stuck here in rehab for a little while. It's nice to get out on a holiday."

"Come sit down," I said. "We're just finishing up." I led them over to the table. "Sit wherever you'd like."

"You better show me where," Chuck said.

"Sorry," I said. I pulled out a chair and led his hand to the back of it. "You can sit right here."

"Thank you, little lady."

"Can I get you something to drink?" my father asked the men. "Wine? Beer?"

"I'll have some wine," Joel said.

"None of that fancy stuff for me," Chuck said. "I'll take a Bud if you got one."

My father brought over a can of beer and a glass of white wine. "It's probably sacrilege for an Italian not to serve a Chianti, but I'm supporting the local economy. This vino is called Serenity, it's from the Sanders Winery in Pahrump."

Joel took a sip. "It's good. Thank you."

"It's got a touch of pear and sweet jasmine," my father said, walking back to the kitchen. "I rather like it."

"You talked me into it," Chuck said. "You could be a pitchman for the stuff. I better try some."

"How about you, sweetie?" my father asked. "A little vino?"

"I'll have a glass," I said. *Or maybe the bottle,* I thought.

My father poured two more glasses of wine and carried them over to the table, then retrieved the cloth-lined basket of rolls and brought them over as well. "Hot from the oven. We've got everything but the turkey."

"Don't hold back on the bird," Chuck said. "It's not Thanksgiving without the bird."

As my father brought the platter over, Chuck raised his nose and breathed in the aroma. "Oh, that is heaven," he said. "I'm drooling like one of ol' Pavlov's canines. Let's eat."

"After we say thanks," my father said. He took my hand and Joel's shoulder. The rest of us took the hands of those next to us. "Kim, will you say grace?"

"Thank you," I said. I bowed my head. "Dear Lord, we are thankful for this day to consider all we have to be grateful for. We are grateful for this food and the abundance of it. We are grateful to be together . . ." Suddenly I could feel emotion rise in my throat. "Bless our health. Amen."

"Amen," everyone said.

"Let's get eating," my father said. "White meat is on the side closest to you, Chuck, dark on the other."

"I like them both. You mind dishing up for me, dear?" he asked me.

"Not at all. What would you like?"

"A little of everything," he said. "To begin with."

I dished up his plate and set it in front of him and he again breathed in deeply. "I have died and gone to heaven. Those are real mashed potatoes, aren't they? Not the fake, pearl kind."

"I mashed them myself."

"And the corn. Is it hand shucked?"

"What?"

"It's a line from a Bill Murray movie," Joel said, smiling. "Don't answer him. It will just encourage him."

"And is that divine smell pecan-crusted sweet potatoes?"

"You can smell that?"

"Oh yes. When my eyes went, my nose took over. I can almost read with my nose."

"Chuck's been in the veterans hospital for about three months," my father said. "He's waiting for a liver transplant."

"That's why I got this funny belly," he said, rubbing his stomach. "It's called ascites. It's caused by buildup of fluid in the abdomen. They pump it out, and it comes back a week later." He turned toward my father. "You know, it occurred to me the other day that I might finally be getting old."

"You're only as old as you think you are," my father said.

"I think I'm four hundred years old."

"How long do you have to wait?" I asked.

"Probably a month after I die," he said. "At my age, I'm not exactly a high priority on the donor list. And it is the VA."

His last comment especially bothered me. "Where's your family?" I asked. I immediately regretted the question as a look of pain flashed across his face.

"They can't be bothered with an old man like me."

There was an awkward silence. I took a sip of wine, then said, "My father said you served in the Korean War."

"No," he said. "It wasn't a war. It was a police action. That's what Truman called it."

"But you served in Korea," my father said.

"Yes, sir."

I turned to Joel. "And you served in Iraq?"

"Yes. Iraq and Afghanistan. Afghanistan is where the war ended for me. Our Humvee drove over an IED. I was the lucky one. I lost a few body parts, but everyone else lost their lives."

Lucky hadn't crossed my mind. "You're from Vegas?"

"Originally I'm from Huntsville. But my wife and I lived here with her mother before I left for Iraq." His face fell. "But we're getting divorced."

I could see the pain saying this brought him. "She filed for divorce when she found out that all of her husband wasn't coming back."

"I'm so sorry."

"I mean, I can see how it would be hard. I lost more than my limbs." He hesitated. "It's not what she signed up for."

"You're being too kind to her," I said.

He looked me in the eyes. "I've seen a lot of hurt in this world. Can you be too kind?"

I couldn't answer.

Joel took a deep breath. "Anyway, I'm thankful that we didn't have any children before I left. Way things came down, that would have messed them up either way, you know? Half of their father comes home."

"I'm sorry," I said.

He forced a smile. "So your father says you don't live in Vegas."

"I've been living in Denver for the last three and a half years."

"It's too cold in Denver," Chuck said. "That's why they call it the Mile High City."

"They call it the Mile High City because it's a mile above sea level," my father said.

"That too."

"I read that the high in Denver yesterday was six degrees," I said. "There were five-foot snow-drifts."

"That's inhuman," Chuck said. "Like back in

fifty in Pusan. The ground was so frozen we had to light flares just to plant tent stakes. Could I have some more of those sweet potatoes? And a little more corn bread stuffing?"

"Of course," I said, taking his plate. As I returned it Joel said, "Your father told us that you're an author."

"I'm an *aspiring* author," I said. "My day job is doing the paperwork at a car dealership."

"What dealership?" Chuck asked.

"Lexus."

"Lexus makes a fine car," he said. "I always wanted one of their little sports cars, but couldn't swing it."

Joel continued. "So have you written some books?"

"One. It still needs to be edited. I'm trying to find a publisher, or an agent, but I keep getting rejections."

"I hear that happens to all writers," Joel said mercifully. "A few weeks ago I saw this author on PBS. He said he had a collection of dozens of rejection letters. After he sold his first million books, he wrote each of the publishers who had rejected him and sent them a copy of the *New York Times* bestseller list with his book at number one and a letter telling them how much money they had lost so far. Then he had all his rejection letters framed."

"I'm still working on my collection," I said.

"What's your book about?"

"It's a holiday romance about this lonely woman who meets a man who is dreading going to all his holiday events alone, so he asks her if she would like to pretend to be a couple."

"Pretend?" Chuck asked.

"Yes. They're the only ones who know their relationship's not real."

"And they fall in love?" Chuck said.

"It's a love story," my father said. "Of course they fall in love. If it was a thriller, they'd shoot each other."

"It sounds interesting," Joel said. "I'd read it."

"You'd read a romance?" I asked. "I see you as more of a Brad Thor or Lee Child reader."

He smiled. "Actually, I do like a good thriller, but I'm open to other genres. If a writer's got a good style."

"She's got a great style," my father said. "She's going to a writers' conference in a couple weeks. She'll get a chance to meet some agents and hopefully sell her book."

"That's really great," Joel said. "I hope things work out."

"I don't know if I'm really going," I said. "I mean, I looked at it, but it was kind of out of my price range."

"She's going," my father said.

I didn't say anything.

"Well, it sounds like a lot of fun," Joel said. "When you have your first book signing, I'll be the first in line."

"You're very sweet," I said.

"The truth is, you could sell books just from your author photo. You're very pretty."

I was a little taken aback. "Thank you."

There was an awkward silence. Joel blushed, then said, "I'm sorry, ma'am. I didn't mean to embarrass you."

"No. That was very sweet."

He still looked embarrassed. "I can't believe I put my foot in my mouth when there's all this delicious food I should be eating instead."

"What can I get you?" I asked.

"Well, I'd give an arm and a leg for some more of that sweet potato casserole."

The whole table went quiet. Then he suddenly laughed. "Wait, I already did."

What a beautiful man, I thought.

"Best Thanksgiving dinner I've ever had," Chuck said, patting his stomach.

"You're being kind," my father replied.

"Since when has anyone accused me of that?" he asked. "You know me, I'm old enough to speak the truth. My first wife was a horrible cook. The second one wouldn't cook. I don't know which was worse."

Joel and I smiled at each other.

"I'll get some coffee," my father said. "Any takers?"

"I'd like some," Joel said. "With a little milk."

"Me too," I said.

While my father made the coffee I brought the pies over to the table.

"What'ya got there?" Chuck asked. "It smells like pies."

"Right again. Pumpkin and pecan."

"I would like both, please."

I turned to Joel. "What would you like, Joel?"

"May I have some pecan, please?"

"Of course. Would you like it à la mode?"

"Yes, ma'am."

"Heated up?"

"No, cold is good. I don't like melted ice cream."

"I'm the same way," I said.

"It's all the same once it hits the stomach," Chuck said.

"I don't know why people say that," my father said.

I served pie to the two men, then took a sliver of both kinds for myself. After coffee, the men watched the Dallas Cowboys and the Washington Redskins football game while I did the dishes. I'm not saying they left me to do them—actually everyone offered to help, especially Joel, whom I practically had to push out of the kitchen. My father was even more difficult to dissuade. I got him out of the kitchen by telling him that he was being rude leaving his guests alone in the living room.

"They're watching the game," my father said. "They don't need me."

"Go," I said. "You always watch football on Thanksgiving. Besides, I don't want anyone in my kitchen."

When he finally realized that I wasn't going to back down, he grabbed a beer and walked out, muttering, "It's my kitchen."

The truth was I wanted to be alone. And I wanted them to enjoy themselves. All three of them were suffering more than I ever had. I guess I had found something to be grateful for after all.

Chapter
Eight

Back to Colorado again. The most certain exiles are those that are self-imposed.

Kimberly Rossi's Diary

The men's shuttle from the hospital came to pick them up a little after seven-thirty. Dad talked the driver into staying for some pie, then sent the pumpkin pie back to the hospital with Chuck. Before leaving, Joel shook my hand.

"Thank you for everything, ma'am. I thought today was going to be miserable, but it wasn't. The food was excellent, and the company was even better. It was a real pleasure meeting you. Maybe we could get a coffee when you're back in town."

"I'd like that," I said. "And thank you."

"For what?"

"For your sacrifice for your country. For us."

"It was my honor, ma'am."

I furtively glanced at his broken body. "God bless," I said.

After they were gone, my father came back to the kitchen and made a turkey sandwich from the rolls and leftover turkey, heating up some gravy in the microwave to dip his sandwich in. Then he sat down at the table next to me.

"Best part of Thanksgiving," he said. "Leftovers."

"I think we have enough to last until Christmas."
I looked at him. "Your friends were nice."

"Yeah. Chuck can be a bit cantankerous, but that comes with age and pain. He's a good man. And he's dying. Did you notice his skin was yellow?"

"Yes."

"That's his liver failing."

"But he said he's going to get a transplant?"

My father shook his head. "He says that, but he's too old for a transplant. They wouldn't waste the organ. Besides, he'd never survive the operation."

"How long does he have?"

"A couple of weeks ago I asked his doctor. He said he doesn't have a crystal ball, but he'd be surprised if he makes it to Christmas."

"So this was his last Thanksgiving."

My father nodded. "That's why I invited him."

"And Joel? I can't believe he doesn't hate his wife. I don't even know her, and I hate her."

"Don't be too quick to judge," my father said. "We all mourn loss in different ways. But you're right. Joel's an amazing young man." He looked at me for a moment. "I think he was taken with you."

"I'm sure he's lonely."

"I'm sure he's lonely for female companionship."

"Maybe we'll get a coffee. It's the least I can do."

My father shook his head. "No, don't go out with him out of sympathy. That would be wrong."

"Then how about out of friendship?"

"Friendship is good. If he's attracted to you, he might not be able to handle that. But it's good to let him make that decision. Besides, you never know how these things can go."

"You approve of him?"

"Oh yes. Even with missing parts, he's still more of a man than most of the men I know."

"Or the ones I've been with?"

"He's ten times the man Marcus was. Is. But that's setting the bar low."

"I can't argue with that," I said. "I'm glad you invited them. This morning I couldn't think of a single thing to be thankful for. Now I could make a list."

"Good," he said. "There are bigger problems than ours."

"Cancer is a big problem."

"It can be," he said. "But I'm going to be okay. And I still wouldn't trade my problems with either of theirs."

I nodded slowly. "What you said, about the writers' conference. I'm not going."

"Of course you are."

"No, I'm not. It's too expensive. And I'm not going to take any money from you."

"That's not your decision."

I laughed. "How is it not my decision if I'm going to go or not?"

"It's not your decision whether I give you money or not."

"What, you're going to make me go?"

"No, but I already paid for it. Including meeting with an agent. I got you two of them in case you don't like one of the agents."

I was stunned. "You signed me up for the conference?"

"You said you wanted to go, so I booked it as your Christmas present."

"How did you even know where to find it?"

"It's not the Holy Grail. I just searched for a writers' retreat at the Mistletoe Inn with H. T. Cowell." He looked somewhat proud of himself. "I gave them a credit card and it's nonrefundable. So no, you don't have to go, but you'll waste a lot of my money if you don't."

"Dad, you've got to get that money back."

"They were very specific about there being no refunds."

I was speechless. "That's not fair."

"What's not fair? It's my money, I can do what I want with it. And what I want is for my girl to pursue her dream."

"Dad . . ." I stopped, overcome with emotion. "I wish you hadn't done that."

"Look, if you really want to make me miserable, stop living. That's when I *will* want to die. Remember, it's about the punctuation."

"You sound like my high school English teacher."

"Whatever works," he said.

I spent the next two days with my father pretending that nothing was wrong. It was a pleasant fiction and I was happy until I flew out Sunday morning and reality returned. I started to tear up on the way to the airport. My father didn't say anything about me crying but reached over and took my hand.

As my father dropped me off he got out of the car and we hugged. "Remember," he said, "the best years of our lives are ahead of us. And it's time that you realized that dream of yours. The world is waiting for you."

"Thanks, Dad." When we parted I said, "Take good care of yourself."

"I always do," he said.

As soon as I got inside the airport I broke down in tears.

Chapter
Nine

*Why is it that, so often, those with
the least are the most eager to give?*

Kimberly Rossi's Diary

For the next few weeks I spent most of my time after work revising my novel, but you can only do that so many times before the words all start to look the same. It's simple psychology. After you've driven the same route a thousand times, you stop noticing the landscape. My father was right, a retreat would be helpful. Still, after he had sacrificed so much, the pressure of going to the conference was heavy. What if it didn't work out? How would I tell him that no one wanted my book?

To add pain to my misery, Rachelle and her new boyfriend were now talking marriage and I was suddenly her confidant. It was like she got some sadistic pleasure out of telling me how happy she was and, twisting the knife, how certain she was that I would someday find someone nice as well, managing to wrap her condescending tone in faux magnanimity.

As the days went on, my father's cancer was always in the back of my mind, lurking in the shadows like a stalker. I was relieved when he finally had his first appointment with an oncologist at the VA a week after I'd flown home. He called me that night after work.

"What did he say?" I asked.

"Actually, it was a cancer care team," he said. "And, generally speaking, they were pretty positive about things. Other than the cancer, I'm quite healthy, so surgery is an option. They're recommending a partial colectomy followed by some chemo."

"When are they going to operate?"

He paused. "Sometime next year. Maybe next February."

"*Maybe* next February? They're making you wait?"

"It's just the way it is. They're backlogged."

"That's too long," I said. "It could spread. There's got to be something we can do. Someone we can talk to."

"There's no need to get so upset. If it was more urgent, I'm sure they would have scheduled me sooner. They're not going to take chances with someone's life."

"You don't know that," I said. "Bureaucracy kills people. This isn't right. I'm going to make some calls. I'm going to talk to your oncologist."

"I talked to my oncologist," he said. "He said this is what they can do."

"But is it what they *should* do?"

"He said that he'll do all he can. He can't break the rules, but sometimes he can bend them. So stop worrying about me; everything will be okay. You've got a writing retreat coming up. You need to be focused."

"How am I supposed to be focused when I'm worried about you?"

"You just focus on knocking them dead at that retreat. That's what I want."

I sighed. "I'll do my best."

"I love you."

"I love you too, Dad." As I hung up the phone, I wished that I had never told him about the retreat.

Chapter
Ten

*Sometimes there's a fine line between
trepidation and excitement.*

Kimberly Rossi's Diary

The morning of December 10th I parked my car in the long-term parking lot of the Denver Airport and took the shuttle in to the terminal. There wasn't a direct flight from Denver to Burlington, Vermont, so I had a three-hour layover in Detroit, where I ate lunch and wandered through the air-port. In a magazine shop I watched people browse through the books. *How would that be?* I wondered. *To have a book on one of those shelves?*

It was dark when my cab drove up a pine-lined lane to the Mistletoe Inn, each of the trees wrapped with white Christmas lights.

"It looks cozy," I said.

"Yeah," the driver said. "It's a real nice place. Kind of fancy."

The inn was decorated for the season with twinkling, draped garlands running the length of the hotel, glowing against the snow-blanketed backdrop of the deep purple night.

As I got out of the taxi, a young man wearing a long blue wool coat with black piping and a black felt top hat walked up to me. "Would you like help with your bag?"

"No, thank you. I just have the one. It's not heavy."

"No problem; let me get the door for you."

He opened the tall wooden doors and as I walked past him I was embraced by the warmth and ambience of the inn's extravagant lobby. "Greensleeves," played on a harpsichord, faintly reverberated throughout the room. All around the lobby were flickering red candles, and the room was filled with a pleasant scent of cinnamon, clove, and pine.

There was a large Christmas tree next to the check-in counter hung with red baubles and silver icicles and tiny white flickering lights. The lobby walls were paneled with dark wood planks, and black metal carriage lamps hung from the high ceiling.

In the center of the room was a large fireplace with a roaring fire inside. The fireplace's mantel was made of polished dark pine with a garland draped over it, tied with red velveteen ribbons.

In front of the fire were two leather sofas and two red-velvet armchairs, arranged beneath a massive light fixture made of deer antlers. The sofas were occupied by an older couple and two young women, all holding wineglasses.

A few yards in from the door, on a gold easel, was a sign that read:

Romance Writers
Conference
Registration

An arrow, which looked like the nib of a fountain pen, pointed to a table to the right of the check-in counter. The table was occupied by a lone fortyish woman with short auburn hair and thick-rimmed glasses. There was a small line at the hotel's check-in counter so I walked to the registration table. The woman smiled as I approached.

"Hello," she said warmly. "Are you here for the conference?"

"Yes," I said, setting down my bag. "I'm Kim Rossi."

"Rossi, let me look that up." She lifted a two-page roster and slid her index finger down the list, stopping about halfway on the second page. "Rossi," she said. "Kimberly."

"That's me."

"You came clear from Colorado. How was your flight in?"

"It was good," I said.

"Good, good. Let's get you checked in." She handed me a manila envelope with my name handwritten in purple marker on the outside. "This is your conference packet; it has your credentials along with a list of panels and lectures and some other information." Then she lifted a white canvas bag from the floor behind her. "And this is a little welcome gift from the Vermont Tourist Association. It has a brochure with some coupons and a list of things to do in the area.

There's also some locally produced maple syrup and maple candies in there. I should warn you, the maple walnut fudge is addicting."

"Thank you," I said, taking my things. "I'll be careful with the fudge."

"And don't forget, our conference opening reception is tonight at 7 p.m. in the grand ballroom. You won't want to miss it."

"How many are registered for the conference?"

"We have just over a hundred," she said.

A voice behind me asked, "What's the male-to-female ratio?"

I turned around. Standing behind me was a beautiful woman about my height and maybe a year or two younger. She had long red hair that fell past her shoulders, freckled cheeks, and green eyes that were unusually brilliant.

"Unfortunately, the odds are in favor of the men," the woman said. "There are only seven men enrolled."

"May the odds be ever in your favor," I said to the woman.

She looked at me. "That's from . . . wait, I know this."

"*Hunger Games*," I said.

She clapped. "Yes! Are you Suzanne Collins?"

I looked at her blankly, wondering if she was serious. "I'm sorry, I'm not."

"I'm sorry I'm not her either." She put out her hand. "My name is Samantha."

I took her hand, still not sure what to think of her. "Kim Rossi."

"What kind of name is Rossi?" she asked.

"It's Italian."

"I love Italian," she said.

The woman at the table said, "Let me find your registration, Samantha. What's your last name?"

"McDonald."

"Samantha McDonald." She looked through her papers. "Here you are." She handed her a packet and canvas bag, reciting the same spiel she had for me, ending with, "The opening reception is tonight at seven in the grand ballroom. Enjoy the conference."

I thanked the woman again, then walked over to the line at the check-in counter. The line had shortened and there was just one couple ahead of me. Samantha followed me over. "Is this your first time at one of these writers' conferences?" she asked.

"No. But it's my first time at this one."

"This is my first writers' conference. I'm a little nervous."

"You don't need to be nervous," I said. "It's fun to be with other writers. They're all in the same boat as you."

"Are you from Vermont?"

"No. Colorado."

"Oh, we're neighbors. I'm from Montana."

"Are there many writers in Montana?"

"Tons. It's Montana—what else are you going to do?"

"Next, please," the man at the check-in counter said.

"Excuse me," I said.

I got my room key, then, as I turned to go, Samantha stopped me. "Are you going to the party tonight?"

"I was planning on it."

"Do you want to go together?"

"Sure," I said. "I'll meet you here at seven."

"I'll be here with bells on," she said.

I'm not sure why I had agreed so quickly. She seemed a little crazy. But she also seemed kind of fun. Besides, I hated being alone at parties.

My room was nice—well designed, modern, but quaint. In the center of the room was a tall, king-sized bed with an antique headboard of dark oak and tufted dark-brown leather. The bed had a thick, greenish-tan duvet cover with matching pillow shams, along with several smaller decorative pillows.

On the wall opposite the bed was a large, rectangular mirror in an elaborate wooden frame. The mirror made the room look larger.

I sat down on the foot of the bed and opened up my conference packet. Next to several loose forms and registration papers were stapled pages with a schedule of events. I found a pen next to the telephone, then started down the list, checking or circling some of the classes that interested me.

LIST OF PRESENTATIONS AND EVENTS

MEET AND GREET
Monday evening, 7 p.m., Grand Ballroom. Credentials required.

Check.

OPENING SESSION
Tuesday, 9–9:45 a.m. Presenter: Jill Tanner, Chairperson of the Mistletoe Inn Writers' Conference Committee, and Kathryn Nebeker, this year's Vice Chairperson of content.

Check.

DAILY GROUP WORKSHOPS
Tuesday, 10–10:45 a.m.
Wednesday–Saturday 9–9:45 a.m.

Important Note: You will meet each day with your workshop group. You have been preassigned to a group of 10 writers. Please check your packet for a yellow sheet with your designated group letter.

Check. I found an 8 1/2-by-5 1/2 yellow sheet inside the envelope. Printed on it was a large letter *C* with the instructions that the group would be meeting in the Maple Room. I went back to the list of events.

TWITTER IN YOUR FACE(BOOK)
Building a community of readers through social media.

Maybe. I made a check by it.

HOW NOT TO GET AN AGENT
Famous New York literary agent Laurie Liss shares the 5 things not to do when pitching an agent.

Absolutely. I circled it.

CLOTHES MAKE THE *RO*-MAN-*CE*
Dressing (and undressing) your characters for success.

Probably not. Maybe. I put a check by it.

THE CHANGING FACE OF ROMANCE
From *Romeo and Juliet* to *Love Story* to *Bridges of Madison County* to *Fifty Shades of Grey*: Where the romance world is going next.

Sounds interesting. Circled it.

PUTTING THE *ROME* BACK IN ROMANCE
Creating the perfect Italian setting for an Italian love story.

No. I'm Italian, but my book's not set in Italy.

THE LIMOUSINE LIFESTYLE OF THE BESTSELLING AUTHOR
(Wednesday only) Mega-Selling Author Catherine McCullin recounts her career as one of the world's most celebrated romance writers.

Of course. Circled it.

AGENT SPEED DATING
Fifteen minutes to pitch your book to a real literary agent. (Additional fee required.) Reservations must be made before 1 p.m. on Tuesday. Sessions held Wednesday, Thursday, Friday only. Reservation form is included in packet. First come, first served.

This was what my father had paid for. Twice. I circled it.

FROM WALMART TO HOLLYWOOD
Bestselling Author Deborah Mackey talks about her rocket-like rise from retail store

clerk to international bestselling author (via Skype).

Maybe. Don't like the Skype part. Sounds like she's phoning it in.

WHIPS AND CHAINS
(No, nothing exciting.) How to endure the stress and pressures of a sweatshop publishing house.

Probably not.

BORING PUNCTUATION!
How to use punctuation (and not use it) to strengthen your stories.

Definitely boring.

VAMPS AND VAMPIRES
Tips for writing sizzling paranormal romances.

No interest in vampires whatsoever. Was once married to one.

BARE FEET AND BUGGIES
Writing your Amish love story.

Same as vampires. I wonder if anyone has written a vampire-Amish romance. If not, it will happen.

LIVING THE DREAM
Author David Bready shares his secrets to breaking down the walls to the publishing world.

Sounds good. Never heard of Bready. But he's published . . .

THE EYES HAVE IT
Facial gestures that say more than words.

I could use that.

E-LECTRIC
How to heat up the Internet with your e-book.

Yes.

MAKING A 6-FIGURE SALARY ON 4-FIGURE BOOK SALES
How to make a lucrative living as a midlist author.

Quit the dealership to write? Okay.

CHOPPING THE WRITER'S BLOCK
How to keep writing when the words stop coming.

Definitely need this.

CLOSING KEYNOTE: WHY I STOPPED WRITING
H. T. Cowell.

I circled this a half dozen times. It was the first time that I saw what Cowell was speaking about, which frankly was exactly what I wanted to hear. Maybe what the whole world hoped to hear.

I set the conference material on the night table next to my bed and lifted my suitcase onto a luggage stand. I unzipped my case and took out my manuscript. I looked at it, then put it back in my suitcase. There was a little more than an hour before the reception so I set the alarm on my phone for fifteen minutes, then lay back on the bed. As I closed my eyes my phone rang. It was my father.

"Hi, Dad. How are you feeling?"

"I'm good," he said. "So are you there yet? At the inn?"

"Yes. I'm in my room."

"How is it?"

"It's beautiful. The whole inn is beautiful."

"The whole state is beautiful," he said. "I've always thought of Vermont as one of the most beautiful states. Especially when the leaves turn."

"I didn't know you'd been here."

"Mom and I went there on our honeymoon. We went on one of those fall leaves tours. It was unforgettable."

I hated the idea that my mother had been here. It was like discovering snakes in Eden. "It's all covered in snow now," I said.

"I'm sure that's beautiful too. So is anything going on tonight or do you get time to rest?"

"There's an opening-night reception in about an hour."

"Then I better let you get ready. I just wanted to make sure you had made it safe. Have a good time. And would you bring me back some of that real Vermont maple syrup? I don't know if it's the season, but there are places where you can see them boiling down the sap into syrup."

"I'll bring you some. I think there's some in my welcome bag."

"Thanks, baby. Have a good time. I love you."

"I love you too," I said. "Take care of yourself."

I tossed my phone onto the bed, then turned around and looked at myself in the mirror across from me. I always felt bloated after flying. "You look like roadkill," I said out loud. I undressed, then went in to shower.

I turned on the water and a cloud of steam filled the small room. I sat down in the porcelain claw-foot tub beneath the spray and closed my eyes. As I lay there thinking about my father, I felt a panic attack coming on. "He's going to be okay," I said to myself. "Everything will be okay. Our best years are still ahead of us."

Chapter
Eleven

*Is it favor or folly that we don't know
how far we are from our dreams?*

Kimberly Rossi's Diary

The conference's opening reception was held in the inn's grand ballroom, which, according to the program material, was also where the conference's most popular sessions would take place, including the opening session in the morning and the final keynote speech by Mr. Cowell.

I walked into the lobby a few minutes after seven. I looked around for Samantha but didn't see her, so after waiting for a little while, I went inside to see if she was already there. The lights inside the ballroom were partially dimmed and there was music playing from a set of speakers attached to an iPod. The room wasn't particularly crowded. There were about fifty or sixty people, mostly clustered in small, intimate groups.

The woman at the registration desk was correct in her estimated male-to-female ratio, as the vast majority of the attendees were women. I looked around for Samantha but couldn't find her.

In the center of the room were tables with hors d'oeuvres. I hadn't eaten since lunch in Detroit, so I took a plate and began to fill it with food: quiche, deviled eggs, sausage-stuffed mushrooms, bacon-wrapped water chestnuts, and dates with blue cheese centers.

Next to the food was a round table with beverages: sodas, eggnog in a large crystal punchbowl, and prepoured glasses of wine.

As I lifted a glass of red wine, a man, balding with a narrow, ruddy face, walked up to me. He wore denim jeans and an oxford shirt with a herringbone tweed jacket with leather elbow patches, the kind that Marcus used to wear while teaching. He was also holding a glass of wine. I couldn't tell if his face was red because he'd been skiing or because he'd been drinking.

He furtively glanced down at my bare ring finger as he stuck out his hand, his close-set eyes fixed on me. "Hi, I'm John Grisham."

I set down my drink to shake his hand. "No, you're not."

An eager grin crossed his face. "I know, but it gets your attention, doesn't it? I'm David." He gripped my hand a little too firmly and held it longer than was comfortable.

"I'm Kimberly."

"Hi, Kimberly. I'm sure you hear this often, but you're a very attractive woman."

Not as often as I'd like, I thought. "Thank you."

"Are you here for the writing seminar?" he asked. It was a dumb question since this was a reception for the seminar.

"Yes. And you?"

"I'm one of the presenters," he said, his voice taking on a slightly lilting tone. "I'm *published.*"

There is a caste system at writers' conferences—a social stratification between the elite and the untouchables, the published and unpublished.

"Congratulations," I said. "That must be nice."

"Yes, it is. What do you do?"

"In real life I'm a finance officer at a car dealership."

"Living the dream," he said sardonically.

"But I'd like to be writing for a living."

"You and everyone else on the planet."

"That's encouraging," I said. "What is your presentation on?"

"It is on exactly what we're talking about—how to get published. Actually my presentation's called *Living the Dream*."

"I saw it on the schedule. You're David . . . Bready." I pronounced his last name like *Breedy*.

"It's pronounced Brady," he said quickly. "Like Tom."

"I'm sure you'll have a very popular session."

"It's always a crowded session," he replied. "I pack them in." He lifted a stuffed mushroom from the table and devoured it in one bite.

"So what books have you written?" I asked.

He finished chewing, then said, "I co-wrote one of the Chicken Soup books. *Chicken Soup for the Romance Writer's Soul*."

"I didn't know there was one for that."

"Oh yeah. It's one of the bigger sellers."

"How many Chicken Soup books are there

now?" I asked. "I mean, hasn't it gotten ridiculous? Like, *Chicken Soup for the Bricklayer's Soul*? How many different souls can there be?"

He gazed at me blankly, clearly offended by my question.

"What else do you write?" I asked.

"I'm best known for the Death Slayer series. I'm sure you've heard of it."

I looked at him awkwardly. "Death Slayer?"

"*Cave of the Slave Girls, Slaughter Alley, Planet Blood . . .*"

"I'm sorry, I don't read a lot of the . . . death and gore genre."

"I've got a film option on *Planet Blood*," he said. "My agent says Hollywood's going nuts over it."

"Congratulations."

"Thanks, but you know how it is. The publisher's never satisfied. The minute you've finished one book they want to know when the next one will be finished. Got to feed the beast."

"Actually, I don't know how that is," I said. "I'd like to."

"Which is why you should come to my presentation." His mouth twisted. "But honestly, between us, being published has its downside."

"Such as?"

"Fame. Groupies. Women following me back to my hotel after book signings."

"That sounds pretty miserable," I said, nodding.

He either missed my sarcasm or just ignored it.

"Well, believe me, they're not always as lovely as you. So, why don't you come up to my room and I'll show you what I'm working on. I'll even let you read some pages no one else has ever laid eyes on."

I bit my lip. "Thank you, but I think I'll just stay down here and get to know some of the other attendees."

He nodded as if he understood. "I get it. You want to size up the competition."

"I wasn't really thinking of that."

"You should," he said. "Publishing's the most competitive industry on the planet. Breaking into the business today is like safecracking. If you don't know the combination or the bank president, you'll never make it. It's who you know."

"You mean I need to know someone like *you*," I said.

He cocked his head. "Precisely. I know people in the industry. Agents. Editors. People with a say as to what gets published and what doesn't." He leaned forward. "So. Do you want to come up to my room?"

"Tempting, but still no. Thank you."

His jaw tightened. "Suit yourself. Good luck." The last two words sounded more like a threat than a wish. He huffed off. A few minutes later I heard him say to another woman, "Hi, I'm John Grisham . . ."

I took my wine and food over to a vacant table near the side of the room and sat down. As I looked around it seemed like most of the people already knew each other. I felt like a leper. To my relief, it was only a few minutes before Samantha walked into the room. I waved to her and her face lit when she saw me. She walked over to the table. "Oh, I'm so glad you're here. Sorry I'm late. I couldn't get off the phone."

"It's okay," I said. "I just got here too."

"How's the party?"

"It's good." I tilted my head toward David, who was already well into his next pitch. "Stay clear of that guy."

"I know," she said. "His name is David, but he tells everyone he's John Grisham. It's the most pathetic pickup line I've ever heard."

"So you've met him."

"I met him in the hall after I checked in. He's one of the presenters. He's published."

"Yes, he told me."

"He asked me up to his room."

"He asked me too," I said. "What did you say?"

"I said I thought he was kind of old to be hitting on someone my age."

I laughed. "I bet you bruised his ego."

"Crushed it," she said, smiling.

Just then two other women walked over to our table carrying plates of food, a tall redhead and a shorter brunette with heavy makeup. "Excuse

103

me," the redhead said. "Are these seats taken?"

"No. Go ahead."

The women sat across from us. "I'm LuAnne," the redhead said.

"And I'm Heather," said the other.

"I'm Kim," I replied. "And this is Samantha."

"Hi," Samantha said, looking unhappy that the two women had crashed our table.

LuAnne smiled at me. "Is this your first time here?"

"Yes. Is it yours?"

"No. It's my sixth."

"It's my fifth," Heather said. "You could say we're regulars. We noticed that you were talking to David."

"Actually, he was talking to me," I said.

"He was hitting on her," Samantha said.

"Did he invite you up to his room?" LuAnne asked.

"Yes."

"No surprise there," she said. "He always works the pretty new ones."

"The regulars know better," Heather said.

"David's a regular too?" I asked.

"Pretty much," Heather said. "He's one of the few published authors who will consistently come. I think it's getting harder to get published authors. They only found four this year."

"They got Mr. Cowell," I said.

"If he shows," LuAnne said.

I looked at her quizzically. "What do you mean?"

"He has a reputation for booking events and not showing up."

"Like *never* showing up," Heather said. "If he comes, it will be a first."

"He's the reason I came," I said. "Mostly."

"Well, he could surprise us," LuAnne said doubtfully. "So what kind of romance do you write?"

"Kind?"

"Yes. What's your niche? Paranormal? Erotica? Nicholas Sparks wannabe?"

I wasn't sure how to answer. "Just, the usual," I finally said, not sure what that meant.

"How long have you been writing?" Heather asked.

"About six years," I said.

"Same as me," she said.

"How many books have you written?" Samantha asked.

"Counting the one I'm working on, fourteen," LuAnne said.

"Fourteen?"

"I've written twenty-two," Heather said. "But, technically, two of them were novellas."

"And not one of them published," LuAnne said.

Heather glared at her. "I'm published. I've sold almost two thousand copies."

"*Self*-published," LuAnne said dismissively. "Ninety-nine-cent e-books. The book world has radically changed in the last decade. There are no such things as unpublished authors these days."

"That's true," Samantha said. "Amazon has like a billion books."

"I'm still unpublished," I said. I hadn't even considered self-publishing. I wouldn't know where to begin.

LuAnne said, "A few years ago at the Maui Writers Conference, Sue Grafton said, 'You shouldn't even submit a book to an agent until you've written at least five.' "

"I guess that counts me out," I said.

"How many books have you written?" LuAnne asked.

I felt embarrassed. "One."

Both women looked surprised.

"Just one?" Heather asked.

"Yes," I said. "I guess I've had a lot of distractions."

"The truth is," LuAnne said, "writing the book is the easy part. Getting someone to read it is the real trick. There's so much competition and it gets worse every year. The problem is, everyone thinks they have a book in them."

"Which is precisely where it should stay," Heather said. "*In* them."

"I mean, you walk into a bookstore and you think, each one of these books probably sells a few hundred copies, right?" LuAnne said. "Do you know what the average book sells in a bookstore?"

I shook my head. "No."

"One point eight copies. Not even two."

"How do you sell eighty percent of a book?" Samantha asked.

"It's in the aggregate," LuAnne said.

"It's a doggy-dog world out there," Heather said.

"You mean dog-eat-dog world," LuAnne said.

"That's what I said," Heather said.

LuAnne turned to me. "Have you sent your book out to anyone yet?"

"I've sent it to a few publishers, but they just sent back rejection slips."

"You're lucky you even got an acknowledgment," LuAnne said. "Sending directly to publishers is a waste of time. They get more books than they can read just from the agents. They don't have time to look at the nonagented books. It's the weeding process."

"Have you tried sending out to agents?" Heather asked.

"No. I signed up for the speed-dating thing. I hope I can find one here."

"Good luck," she said. "It's brutal out there."

It's brutal in here, I thought.

"There are two kinds of agents who come to these things," Heather said. "The first is the kind who comes for a junket and doesn't really believe they'll find anything. They're the dream killers. They just love shredding your heart into a million tiny pieces.

"Then there are the passive-aggressive agents who realize that no one wants to hear anything bad about their writing, so they just say nice things to everyone, then never call them back. I've had both and I don't know which is worse."

"It depends if you like the bandage pulled off quickly or slowly," LuAnne said.

"There's a third kind, right?" I said.

"A third?" Heather said.

"An agent who is actually looking for a book to sell."

They were both quiet for a moment, then LuAnne said, "It could happen."

Heather nodded. "Could happen."

I felt like a naive child being told that there is no Santa Claus.

The conversation with the two women pretty much crushed any remaining vestige of hope I still had in getting published. I knew there was a lot of competition out there—anyone who's ever walked through a bookstore knows that—but it was soul crushing to realize that for every one of those published authors on the shelf, there were at least a thousand more like me who wanted their job. *How could I have been so naive? How could I have wasted my father's money?*

I downed the rest of my wine, excused myself, and walked out to the lobby. Samantha followed me.

"I don't like those women," she said.

"I didn't like what they had to say," I said.

"What do they know, anyway? It's not like they're famous authors."

I looked at her. "You're right."

She glanced around the mostly vacant lobby. "The night's still young. Want to talk?"

"Sure," I said. The lobby's sofas were unoccupied, so we sat down in front of the fire. That's when I noticed the massive diamond on Samantha's finger. "Are you married?"

"No," she said, looking a little embarrassed. "Chronically engaged."

"What does that mean?"

"It means that I've been engaged for six years."

I nodded, thinking I understood. "You found a man with a commitment problem?"

"It's not him. We'd be on our fifth anniversary if he had his way."

"What's holding you back?"

"The BBD."

"The what?"

"You know, the bigger better deal. I'm waiting for something better to come along. I mean, at some level, we all eventually settle, right? But wouldn't it be awful to belong to someone else when the right one comes along?"

"That's a song by England Dan and John Ford Coley."

"Exactly my point," she said. "It's so common that someone, like this Dan Ford Coleslaw guy, wrote a song about it. It happens all the time. The minute you take a job, you get offered your dream job. The second you commit to a line at the supermarket, the other line speeds up. It's nature's cruel sense of irony. So, I'm waiting."

"That's kind of awful," I said.

"I know, right?"

"I meant for him."

"I'm nice to him," she said. "Believe me, it's not like he's complaining. And on the looks side, I'm like a nine, or, on a bad hair day, an eight point five, and he's barely a six point five, so he knows he's dating up." She nodded. "I'm good to him."

"You are gorgeous," I said.

"Thank you." She sat back. "How about you? Are you married?"

"I was."

"Divorced?"

"Yes."

"How long have you been divorced?"

"We've been separated for almost eight months, but the divorce just went through a couple of months ago."

"Why did it take so long?"

"He was dragging his feet."

"He didn't want the divorce?"

"No, he wanted the divorce. He just didn't want the settlement."

"What a jerk. What happened?"

I sighed. "He was a professor and he fooled around with a few of his students. It was like a big news thing. Nothing like being publicly humiliated and having your broken heart dragged through the media."

"He really is a jerk," Samantha said. "But there is a bright side."

I looked at her incredulously. "How could there possibly be a bright side to that?"

"Fodder," she said. "Think of all the great stuff you could write about it. You could use your loser ex as fodder for all the villains in your books."

"Why would anyone want to read about that? I lived through it and it was miserable."

"That's *exactly* what people *want* to read. Trashy romance is like an emotional garage sale; people get to rummage through other people's junk. Reading how horrible someone else's life is makes them feel better about their own. Why do you think people gossip? That's all romance writers are, the neighborhood gossip in print."

"That's a horrible way to look at writing."

"Horrible or not, you can't fight human nature," she said. "I've written three books. The first one was based on my sister and her ex-husband. I always thought my sister had the perfect marriage. They seemed so happy together. He sent her flowers and Godiva chocolates every week, dream vacations, nice house, the whole grand illusion. He was a successful salesman for some medical appliance company, so he made a lot of money and traveled a lot. Turns out he had a second wife and family in Tulsa."

"You're kidding."

"God-honest truth."

"That's awful."

"My story gets even better. So when the news comes out, the state Attorney General's office brings loser-husband up on bigamy charges. The prosecuting attorney, this really hot guy, is working with my sister on the case. Get this, they fall in love. Now they have this great marriage and he's like so much better looking than Felon."

"Felon?"

"That's what my sister calls her ex."

"Did they have children?"

"With my sister? No. Felon just kept telling her that he wasn't ready. The truth was, he just couldn't afford two families. I mean, he bought braces for Tulsa wife's kids."

"At least they'll have straight teeth when they go to their counseling sessions," I said.

Samantha laughed. "So what's your book about?"

"It takes place during the holidays."

"Smart. Holiday romances are hot. And that's when people are buying books. Go on."

"It's about this woman who has had a string of bad relationships. She works at a downtown travel agency. It's the day after Halloween and she's dreading going through another Christmas alone, when this guy in the mall food court approaches her. She's seen him before, like in the elevator and around the building. He tells her that he hates the holidays because he's alone and has all these parties to go to. He proposes that they pretend to be a couple until Christmas."

"And they fall in love," Samantha said.

"Of course."

"I like the premise," she said. "Is the guy, like, secretly a serial killer or married?"

"No."

"I'm just saying, it would add a lot of drama, if you, like, had this backstory going and you're wondering if she's going to get killed or run into the guy's wife at a Christmas party."

For a moment I was speechless. "No. He's not going to kill her. It's a love story."

"That's good too," Samantha said, standing. "Would you like some more wine?"

I was glad for the reprieve. "Yes. Red, please."

"I'll be right back," she said, walking back into the reception. She returned a moment later carrying two glasses of red wine and handed me one of them. "The party goes on," she said, sitting down. "John Grisham is still at it, going after lucky contestant number three. Someone should tell him he needs a mint."

I grinned. "What's your fiancé's name?"

She grimaced slightly. "Walt. Walt *Berger*. Who wants the last name of *Berger*?"

"Samantha Berger. It's a little unusual, but it's not . . . bad."

"Oh yeah, well, what if I wanted to hyphenate my last name? Or just think of our wedding announcements. McDonald-Berger. That's reason enough not to get married."

I couldn't help but laugh. "I'm sorry. That is unfortunate."

"Yeah, someone will put our announcement on the Internet and mock us."

"So what does Walt do?"

"He's a businessman. He owns a chain of hamburger joints."

For a moment I thought she was joking, but she didn't laugh. "Really?"

"Really," she said. "Berger's Burgers."

"It's a catchy name . . ."

"He says that after we're married he'll name a burger after me." She rolled her eyes. "Now that's an honor."

"McDonald Burger? I think there might be some legal problems with that."

"The Sam Burger," she said. "With special Sam

114

sauce. Whatever that is." She sighed. "I don't know. He's not much to look at. He looks like that Willard Scott guy who used to do the weather on the *Today* show, which is ironic, since Willard Scott was McDonald's first Ronald McDonald clown. But he's a good guy. And I can't say he's not patient."

"Not after six years."

"I keep telling him that Jacob in the Bible had to wait seven years for Rachel."

"Technically, I think it was fourteen years, because he got tricked into marrying the oldest daughter first," I said.

"That's good news," she said. "Not for Jacob, but, I mean, maybe I'll use that."

"You would really make him wait fourteen years?"

"No. After seven years I think the universe is telling me that it's time to settle."

I hoped that she'd never say anything that crass to her fiancé, but I wouldn't be surprised if she already had. She didn't seem to have much of a filter. The massive grandfather clock near the check-in counter chimed.

I glanced at my watch, then said, "I think I'll go to bed."

"All right," Samantha said. "See you at breakfast?"

"I'll be there. Good night."

I walked down the hallway back to my room.

Even though I was still on mountain time, it seemed late to me and I felt tired. I undressed, laid my clothes over the back of a chair, then turned out the light and got into bed. As I lay thinking about what the two women had told us, I wanted to cry. I didn't want to be here. I had wasted my father's money on an unrealistic dream. Money better spent on saving his life. *Why did he make me come?*

Chapter
Twelve

I call it Rossi's Law: the likelihood of having something stuck in your teeth is directly proportionate to the attractiveness of the person you're meeting.

Kimberly Rossi's Diary

The next morning I got up at sunrise and went to the hotel's fitness center. The room was small, with one wall that was all mirrors, presumably to make the space seem less claustrophobic.

There wasn't a lot to work with; a set of barbells, an elliptical, a treadmill, and a stair climber. In the corner of the room a television hung from the ceiling. It was on, tuned to a sports channel.

I draped a hand towel around my neck, then got on the treadmill. I put in my earbuds, turned Josh Groban on my iPod, then turned the treadmill on to a slow jog.

About twenty minutes into my run a man walked in. He was maybe a decade older than me, handsome with short, dark hair and bright blue eyes partially obscured by tortoiseshell-framed glasses. He looked fit, not especially muscular, but nicely proportioned.

He smiled at me as he walked over to the elliptical. Before he got on the machine he turned back to me and said something I couldn't hear. I took out an earbud. "Excuse me?"

"Would you mind if I changed the channel on the television?"

"No, go ahead. I'm not watching."

"Thank you."

I put my earbud back in while he changed the channel from sports to a cooking show, which, I suppose, wasn't what I expected. I would have pegged him as a sports or politics guy.

As he worked out I glanced over at him several times. Once I caught him looking at me. He didn't immediately turn away but smiled pleasantly.

About five minutes before I ended my workout, my towel slipped off my neck, falling to the track. Without thinking I reached for it and, with the machine's momentum, fell to my knees and was promptly ejected off the back of the track, leaving me sprawling on the floor. My iPod flipped across the room.

The man quickly came to my aid. "Are you hurt?"

My face was crimson as I got up on my knees. "Just my pride."

He offered me his hand. "That can be painful too." He helped me up.

"Thank you."

"You're welcome." He stooped over and picked up my iPod. "I believe this is yours."

"Thanks. Again."

"Don't mention it." He returned to his elliptical.

I was too embarrassed to finish my workout, so I threw my towel into a woven basket and walked back to my room. *Smooth, Kim. Real smooth,* I thought. *Way to impress the cute guy.*

Not that it mattered. Chances were that I wouldn't see him again.

I got back to my room at a quarter to eight, which gave me just enough time to shower and dress before breakfast. This time, before I left my room, I put on my wedding ring, just in case I encountered John Grisham again. In the dining room, Samantha was already sitting at a table with a plate of food. She looked pretty.

"Morning, sunshine," she said as I walked over.

"Good morning. What's good?"

"Everything I've tried so far. It's buffet-style. Personally, I'm into the French toast sticks." Her plate was loaded with French toast covered in powdered sugar. "There's also a guy making omelets. Pretty tasty."

"The omelets or the guy making them?"

"Both. I think he's Cuban. He's got a cute accent."

I walked over to the food tables. She was right; everything did look good, including the omelet guy. I took an orange, a small bowl of oatmeal—which I loaded with walnuts, brown sugar, and raisins—grabbed a coffee and creamer, and carried everything back to the table. Samantha had powdered sugar on her lips.

"So after you went back to your room last night," she said, "I went back into the party to do some reconnaissance. A lot of these people are like writers' conference junkies. They all go to the same conferences and hang out."

"That explains why they all seem to know each other."

"The good thing is that everyone agreed that this is their favorite conference. And there's a betting pool on whether your boyfriend is going to show up or not. They're giving two-to-one odds that he's a no-show."

"My boyfriend?"

"Cowell."

"Oh," I said, feeling awful to be reminded of that possibility. I took a bite of oatmeal, then said, "I can't believe that he might not come."

"If he doesn't, we've definitely got grounds for a lawsuit," Samantha said. "Walt's got a good lawyer."

We ate for a while longer, then Samantha glanced down at her watch. "It's almost time. We need to go if we want good seats."

I quickly downed my coffee, then stood. "Let's go."

"Did you bring the manuscript you plan to work on?"

"No. Do I need it?"

"Well, yeah," she said. "It was in the instructions. Go get your manuscript and I'll save us some seats."

With that she took off and I walked back to my room to get my book. My one pathetic, measly book.

Chapter
Thirteen

The conference has begun.

Kimberly Rossi's Diary

The grand ballroom was now brightly lit and filled with chairs. Perry Como Christmas music was playing over the sound system as I walked in, and a crowd of conference attendees, probably double what had been at the evening's reception, milled about visiting or hunting for seats. I spotted Samantha standing near the middle of the third row waving at me. I had to slide past a long line of knees to reach her.

"Good thing I came when I did," she said. "These people are serious about saving places. I sat in one chair and a woman yelled at me. These were the last good seats left."

"Thank you for saving them," I said, taking my seat.

"No worries," she said.

We still had ten minutes before the presentation, so I opened my packet and rooted through it. "Have you looked through all this stuff?" I asked.

"Yes."

"Do you know anything about these work-shops?"

"Just what I read in the packet." She lifted her own program. " 'You will meet daily with the same designated group of writers, where you will share, discuss, and critique your works.' "

"That sounds painful," I said.

"All artists must suffer," Samantha said. "It is the artist's blood that lubricates the rails of artistic expression."

"Where did you hear that?"

"I just made it up."

"That's pretty good."

"Thank you," she replied. "What group are you in?"

"C."

She frowned. "I'm in F. As in *failure*."

"They're groups, not grades."

"I want to be in the same group as you. Do you think they'd let me switch?"

"It doesn't hurt to ask." I glanced around. "If you can find someone to ask."

Samantha looked around the room for a moment, then said, "That woman up there looks important. Hold my seat." She made her way out of our row and walked up to a woman who was standing next to the stage. They spoke only briefly before Samantha turned and walked back. She looked distraught. "That hurt to ask," she said, sitting.

"What did she say?"

"She said they positively don't allow changes."

"It's just one class a day," I said.

"Which roughly equates to one-quarter of the conference," Samantha said.

"Maybe the F group is the place to be."

"Yeah, right."

Suddenly the music stopped and the room lights dimmed, leaving just the stage bathed in light. The crowd quieted in anticipation as a middle-aged woman in a satin periwinkle business suit walked out to a lectern in the center of the stage.

She tapped the microphone, then leaned forward. "Good morning, writers, and welcome to the Mistletoe Inn Writers' Conference. My name is Jill Tanner and I am this year's conference chairperson. We've spent an entire year putting together what we think is the finest schedule of classes and presentations in the country, with one sole objective, to help you reach your goal of becoming a successful published author."

The audience broke out in applause. She waited for the room to quiet before she continued.

"Never degrade yourself by saying you're *just* a romance writer, for nothing is out of the realm of a romance writer. Romance can take place in mystery, politics, science fiction, fantasy, and horror. Indeed, it's the core of nearly all writing. It is the genre of some of the greatest writers of all time: Shakespeare, Austen, and Hemingway. If the public does not take the genre seriously it's only because too many romance writers don't take it seriously. There are good romance writers and bad romance writers and fifty shades of gray between them."

The audience chuckled at the allusion.

The woman smiled. "A little aside: I met a writer—I swear I'm not making this up—who was writing a spicy Amish romance called *Fifty Shades of Hay*. God is my witness, I couldn't make that one up."

The audience laughed again.

"But as I was saying, there are good romance writers and there are bad romance writers. A good romance writer is one who opens up our hearts to the possibility of love. Every year more than two billion dollars' worth of romance novels are sold worldwide. In America alone, more than sixty-four million people will read at least one romance this year. That number has risen steadily each year since we began holding this conference sixteen years ago.

"What this tells me is that we live in a world hungry for love. You, the world's future romance authors, are the providers of the nourishment this world needs. On behalf of the Mistletoe Inn Writers' Conference Committee, we wish you well with your writing and the best of luck on your publishing journey. Now go forth and change the world."

The crowd broke out in wild applause. As she left the stage another woman walked out. It was the same woman whom Samantha had approached.

"Good morning. I'm Kathryn Nebeker, this year's vice chairperson of content. Hopefully you all have your registration packets with you. If you do, please hold them in the air."

We all held up our packets.

"Good. I see most of you have them. One of the things that makes the Mistletoe Inn Writers' Conference such a success is our unique format. We've been told that there is a writers' conference in California that is now trying to *copy* our format. You know what they say about imitation being the sincerest form of flattery, but we writers have another name for it: plagiarism."

Everyone laughed.

"At any rate, part of what makes our conference unique is our daily workshops. These workshops allow one-on-one time with our experienced facilitators and your fellow writers, giving you the chance to improve and develop your work right here at the conference.

"If you look inside your packets you will find a yellow half sheet of paper that looks like this." She held up a yellow page with a large letter *A* printed on it in black. "Your page will have a letter that indicates which workshop you will be attending each day with the location of where you will meet. I cannot overemphasize that it is vital that you attend the workshop to which you have been assigned. Just this morning I had someone come to me to request a change of workshops. This late in the game we cannot accommodate changes."

I glanced over at Samantha, who was staring at the woman hatefully. "Witch," she whispered.

"If for some reason you do not have your card in your packet, we have posted your name with your group letter on papers right outside these doors.

"Again, we are very happy to have you here and I echo the words of Jill, our president, and say, writers, go forth and change the world. Best of luck and enjoy the conference."

The crowd again applauded. As she walked away, the room lights went up and the Christmas music came back on. We all stood and began filing out to our workshops.

"I hate that woman," Samantha said.

"She's just trying to keep things running smoothly," I said.

"She doesn't have to be such a witch about it."

"Where does your group meet?" I asked.

"Probably in the men's room."

"Give it a chance," I said. "After the workshop I'm going to the presentation on How Not to Get an Agent. How about you?"

"I wrote that down too," Samantha said. "Want to get lunch after?"

"Sure."

"All right. Wish me luck."

"Good luck," I said.

"I'm going to need it," she grumbled as she walked away.

Chapter
Fourteen

It turns out that the ship I passed in the night was headed to the same port. Actually, the same harbor.

Kimberly Rossi's Diary

My workshop was in a small conference room near the grand ballroom. There were a dozen chairs arranged in an oval, and one was occupied by a pleasant-looking woman with gray hair. She wore a name badge with a gold presenter's ribbon. I guessed her to be our group's facilitator.

"Welcome," she said with a slight southern accent as several of us walked in. "This is group C. C as in Calhoun, Carlyle, Carroll, and Collodi. C as in cash cow. If you're in the right place, please take a seat in the circle."

I sat down next to the facilitator, and she began checking our name tags against a list on a clipboard. The only person in the room whom I recognized was Heather, one of the two women I had talked to at the opening reception. She glanced at me and sort of waved. I sort of waved back.

After nearly all the chairs were filled, a man, the only man in our group so far, stepped into the room. To my embarrassment, he was the same man I had seen in the exercise room that morning—the one who had helped me up after my fall.

"Excuse me, is this group C?" he asked from the doorway.

Our facilitator nodded. "Yes, this is C. And what's your name?" she asked, checking her clipboard.

"Zeke," he said. "But I'm not on your list. Jill just told me to come here."

She looked back up. "Jill's the boss. Would you mind shutting the door behind you?"

"Not at all," he said. He pulled the door shut, then came over to the circle. As he took the last vacant chair, I noticed several other women checking him out—some, like Heather, more obviously than others. He didn't seem to notice.

"All right," our facilitator said. "My name is Karen Mitchell, and I will be facilitating this workshop every morning of the retreat. First, a little about me. I worked as an editor for Simon & Schuster Adult Division for about five years before I left to work for Avon, an imprint of HarperCollins, where I work today. What I plan to do with you in this workshop is similar to what I do for my published authors every day."

As she spoke I noticed that an older woman seated across from me kept leaning forward, as if she was having trouble hearing. Then I saw that she wore hearing aids in both ears.

"Before we begin, we're going to be together for a few days, so I think we should get to know each other a little better."

"Excuse me," I said to Karen.

Karen turned to me, looking slightly annoyed by my interruption. "Yes?"

"I'm sorry," I said. "I think this woman might be having trouble hearing." I turned to the woman. "Would you like to change seats?"

The woman nodded emphatically. "Yes," she said, her speech slightly impaired. "I have difficulty hearing."

We both stood and as we exchanged seats the woman touched my arm. "Thank you."

"You're welcome," I said.

As I sat down I noticed the man looking at me. He smiled approvingly.

"Okay, writers, onward. As I was saying, I'd like to begin by getting to know all of you a little better. I know how writers like to talk, especially about themselves, so you can do that on your own time. Right now you have two minutes to tell us your name, how long you've been writing, what you're working on now, and what you're most proud of. And be aware," she said, lifting her phone, "I will be timing you. Let's begin with you, darlin'." She nodded to the young woman at her left who wore granny glasses and a peach-colored dress that could have doubled as a tent. I pegged her as one of those sweet timid gals who wrote Amish love stories. She looked terrified.

"Me?"

"Yes, darlin'. Go right ahead."

Still nothing.

"Is this your first writers' retreat?" Karen prodded.

She nodded. "Yes, ma'am."

"Let's begin with your name."

For a moment I thought the woman might faint from fright. "I'm Marci," she squeaked. "I've been writing for about fourteen years, ever since I was fifteen. I'm currently writing a book called *Gone with the Sin*. It's kind of a naughty love story set during Civil War times."

Didn't see that coming.

"I don't know if I'll ever publish it. My father's the pastor at the First Methodist Church of the Lamb in High Point, North Carolina. He wouldn't be very happy with me if he read it."

"We'll address that later," Karen said. "And what are you most proud of?"

"I don't mean to boast, but I won a writing contest last year sponsored by the Lions Club."

"Very good," Karen said. "Next . . ."

Honestly I didn't hear many of the other introductions as my mind was elsewhere. Actually it was mostly on elliptical guy who, unlike me, seemed very much interested in what everyone else had to say. When it was his turn to speak he looked around the group. It seemed to me that his gaze lingered a bit on me.

"Okay, this feels like an AA meeting. Hi, my name is Zeke. I'm a writing addict."

The women to both sides of me giggled.

"First, I have some advice for Marci. Daddy doesn't need to know—that's what noms de plume are for. As for my writing, all I really know about the book I'm working on right now is the price: twenty-four ninety-five in hardcover."

Everyone laughed again.

"Oh . . . and what I'm most proud of is my eight years of sobriety."

Everyone clapped.

"Thank you," Karen said. "Hopefully by the end of our retreat you'll have more of your book to share than a price."

"That would be remarkable," he said.

He glanced over at me and I smiled.

The next two women to speak, Adele and Maureen, were friends who had come to the conference together. They were co-writing a para-normal romance about shark vampires who were, to quote Adele, "stud-muffin surfers by day, and toothy good-guy sharks by night who keep the waves safe."

When it was my turn to speak, my mouth went dry. "My name is Kim," I said. "I've written just one book. I mean I've almost written it. It's not completely finished, but I've already amassed an impressive collection of rejection letters."

A few people laughed.

"It's a Christmas romance called *The Mistletoe Promise*."

"Provocative title," Karen said. "Tell us about it."

"It's about a lonely woman who is recently divorced and has had a string of bad relationships. Then during the holidays, she's approached by a man with a proposition: he doesn't want to spend the holidays alone, so he proposes that they pretend to be a couple until December twenty-fourth. Since he's a lawyer, he writes up a contract."

"Interesting premise," Karen said. "I'll be curious to see where you go with that."

"Me too," I said.

This time almost everyone laughed, even though I hadn't meant to be funny. I glanced over at Zeke. He was looking at me, but I couldn't read his expression.

After we finished going around the circle Karen said, "Okay, we're just about out of time. When we meet tomorrow I'm going to have you read a passage from your writing, so pick something that you feel comfortable sharing, hopefully something from the book you're currently working on.

"Also, here at the Mistletoe retreat, we believe in the buddy system. So before we break today I want each of you to find a writing buddy, someone from this group, to work with for the next six days. This buddy is someone you will share your writing with and get a little constructive criticism from before sharing with the rest of us.

"There's an odd number of people in the room, so one of the groups will need to be a threesome, in a strictly nonromantic sense. Since Adele and Maureen are working on the same book, I suggest that the two of you find someone to join you. We have five minutes before we dismiss, so please don't leave until you've found a buddy. I'll see you tomorrow."

We all stood, looking around at each other. Adele and Maureen quickly cornered Marci and I noticed Heather moving in on Zeke when he walked up to me. "It's Kim, right?"

He didn't really need to ask, as I was wearing a name tag.

I always get a little tongue-tied around handsome men. "Yes. I'm Kim."

"Zeke," he said. "I'm the guy from the gym . . ." When I didn't say anything he said, "I helped you when you fell . . ."

"I remember."

"You're okay, right?"

"Yeah. I probably won't need surgery."

He smiled. "Good. Would you like to be my writing buddy?" Before I could answer he added, "If you had someone else in mind, it's all right. No pressure."

I brushed a strand of hair back from my face. "No. I'd like that. Thank you for asking."

"Very good," he said. "I thought the premise of your book sounded really interesting."

138

"Thank you," I said. "And I thought the *price* of your book sounded very . . . reasonable."

He laughed. "I hope so. So I guess our next step is we should plan a time to get together."

"I was just going to my next seminar, but we could meet for lunch." Then I remembered that I had already committed to lunch with Samantha. "Oh wait. I already promised a friend that I'd meet her."

"Later, then?"

"No, why don't you join us? I'm sure she won't mind. We'll be in the dining room."

"Great," he said. "Then I'll see you around noon. I'm looking forward to working together."

As he turned and walked off I noticed a few of the women looking at me. Heather looked utterly dejected.

Lucky me, I thought.

Chapter
Fifteen

The gorgeous man asked to be my writing partner. What critic is it within me that automatically questions his motives or judgment?

Kimberly Rossi's Diary

The next presentation on my schedule was titled How Not to Get an Agent. The presenter was Laurie Liss, one of the principals of Sterling Lord Literistic, a New York literary agency. Liss's claim to fame, among other things, was discovering an unknown, first-time author named Robert James Waller, who wrote a book called *The Bridges of Madison County*, which not only made Waller a kajillion dollars but helped catapult Liss to the big time and earn her a coronation from the *New York Times* as The Queen of Schmaltz.

The truth was I hadn't sent my book to an agent out of ignorance. An agent, I thought, was just another hurdle I could bypass by going directly to the publisher, not realizing that I was in effect dooming my chances, as publishers rarely look at unsolicited manuscripts.

There were about forty other people at the presentation and Samantha and I took our seats near the front of the room. Liss revealed what she called Liss's List, a list of don'ts when trying to find an agent. I scrawled down the five things that drove Ms. Liss "insane."

1. Don't tell me that your husband/wife/ mother/etc. thinks your book is fantastic. Big surprise: they're either biased or don't

want to hurt your feelings and probably both.

2. Don't offer me a bribe, especially a portion of the enormous amount of money you're going to make off your book. I'll just hang up on you. I take a percentage anyway.

3. Don't send me a photo. I don't care what you look like. The other agents in the firm will hang it up on our bulletin board and draw on it with a Sharpie.

4. Don't ever slip pages under a bathroom stall. I will be so offended that you disregarded my privacy that I will use your pages as toilet paper, or at least send them down the toilet and probably clog it, making a huge mess of the bathroom. And yes, this really happened.

5. Don't ever claim to be the "next big thing." You don't know that. I don't know that. No one knows that. It's presumptuous and embarrassing for you.

As we walked out of the session Samantha said, "I wonder if she'd be my agent."

"I thought she was kind of snarky."

"A good agent needs to be snarky," Samantha said. "The snarkier the better. In the publishing world you swim with the snarks."

"At least you know what *not to do* to get her," I said. "Don't follow her into the bathroom."

"How much do you want to bet that someone will still do that at this conference?"

"I wouldn't be surprised," I said. "We are a desperate lot."

"I just wish she had told us the five things we *should* do."

"Number one should be *write a good book,*" I said. "I'm hungry, let's get some lunch."

We returned to the same dining room where we'd had breakfast. I recognized several people from my workshop.

"There's John Grisham," I said.

"He's not really Grisham," Samantha said.

"Yeah, I know that," I said. "I'm just not so sure that he does."

We found an empty table near one of the windows and put our bags on it, then went over to the buffet table. The day's main courses were chicken cordon bleu, sausage lasagna, and vegetarian lasagna. I opted for the chicken and Caesar salad.

I gave the woman at the cash register one of my conference meal vouchers and went back to our table. Samantha was already eating.

"How was your workshop group?" I asked. "As bad as you thought?"

"I've decided the *F* stands for freaks," she said. "Just about everyone but me is into paranormal romance. But it was okay. They gave us playing cards to pair us up with writing buddies." She took a bite of food and I waited for her to finish chewing to continue. "I drew the queen of hearts, which I figured was a good omen. How about you? Did they pair you up with someone?"

"Yes. But we picked our own buddies."

"Did you have any men in your group?"

"Just one," I said.

"We didn't have any. He wasn't that one guy, was he?"

"Which guy?"

"You know, the hot one who's got the whole Clooney thing going? Handsome, cool glasses, a little older."

"You mean Zeke?" I said.

"You know his name?"

"He's in my group. And I met him earlier in the gym."

"I want to meet Zeke."

I cut into my chicken. "You will."

Samantha looked impressed. "I love your optimism. It's quantum physics—you make your own reality. Just throw it out to the universe and it's going to materialize."

"In this case it's going to materialize sooner than you think. He's going to be joining us for lunch. He's my workshop buddy."

Samantha looked at me incredulously. "Clooney's your workshop buddy."

"He's not Clooney, but yes."

"I told you I was in the wrong group. The

closest thing to a man in our group was this one chick who writes werewolf love stories. She looked like one of them."

"Like a man or a werewolf?"

"Both."

"That's mean," I said. "And here's Zeke now. Watch your tongue."

Zeke walked directly up to our table, his hands in his pockets. "Hi."

"Hi," I returned. "Zeke, this is my friend Samantha. Samantha, this is Zeke."

Samantha just stared at him. "You can call me Sam," she said.

"But Samantha is prettier," he replied.

"Samantha's good," she said.

Zeke turned back to me. "Still all right if I join you?"

Before I could answer Samantha said, "Please."

"Thank you." He pulled out a chair and sat down.

"Did you want to get some food?" I asked.

"What are we eating?"

"I'm having the chicken cordon bleu. It's good."

"It looks good. I'll be right back." He stood and walked toward the buffet tables. Samantha's eyes were glued to him the whole way.

"He's better looking than Clooney," she said.

"No one's better looking than Clooney. Why do you say that?"

"Clooney's not real. Who knows how much of what you see is Photoshop."

"He's a movie star. You can't Photoshop movies."

"Of course you can. It's called special effects."

"Clooney isn't a special effect."

"He has a special effect on me."

I grinned. "You're insane."

Zeke returned a few minutes later with a plate of lasagna and vegetables. As he sat down I said, "You changed your mind about the chicken."

"You didn't tell me there was lasagna. I love Italian."

"Kim's Italian," Samantha said.

I wanted to slap her. Zeke just smiled. As he raised a fork to his mouth, Samantha asked, "Where are you from?"

He put his fork down. "I'm originally from Alexandria, Virginia. But more recently I live in Florida."

"Florida," Samantha said. "Beautiful beaches, beautiful weather."

"If you don't mind an occasional hurricane," Zeke said.

"Where in Florida?" I asked.

"Jupiter Island."

"Isn't that where all the movie stars live?" Samantha asked.

"Some," he said. "Burt Reynolds lives there. Tiger Woods lived there. I'm not sure if he still does."

"You must be rich," Samantha said.

I was now positive that Samantha had no filter.

"Not everyone who lives on Jupiter Island is

rich," Zeke said. "Someone's got to mow the lawns and work the 7-Elevens, right?"

Samantha seemed vexed by the concept. "You mow lawns?"

"From time to time," he said.

I moved to change the topic. "Have you been to many writers' conferences?"

"A few," he said. "But this is the first one I've been to in a while."

"How long's a while?"

"A few years. I let my writing go for a while." He took a bite of lasagna.

"Life happens," I said.

"Yes it does," he said.

"What's your last name?" Samantha asked.

I realized that I didn't know what his last name was either.

He finished chewing, then said, "It's Faulkner."

"Faulkner," I said. "Like the author William Faulkner."

"Unfortunately, yes."

"Why unfortunately?"

"Because sharing the same name of a famous author invites comparison, and trust me, I'm no Faulkner. Think of it this way: if your name was Streisand, people would ask you two things— if you're related to Barbra and if you can sing."

"I can see that," I said.

"You could be like that David guy telling everyone he's Grisham," Samantha said.

"I don't know who you're talking about, but Faulkner is really my name."

"It's still a great name," I said.

"What about you?" he asked. "Do you go to many of these things?"

"I've only been to two others. One in San Francisco, the other local, in Colorado."

"You're from Colorado?"

"Yes."

"I'm from Montana," Samantha said.

He glanced at her. "Montana's beautiful. Big Sky Country."

"That's what they say. I mean, we're not really a country, we're a state. Just like the other fifty. But we have a lot of country." She hesitated. "It's kind of confusing."

Zeke looked at her as if trying to figure out whether or not she was being serious. Then he turned back to me. "Where in Colorado are you from?"

"Denver. I used to live in Boulder, but I moved after I got divorced."

"You're divorced," he said. He casually glanced at the diamond on my ring finger. "And the ring is . . ."

"Garlic."

"Garlic?"

"It keeps vampires away."

"Does it work?"

"We'll see," I said.

149

"So this is your first time at the Mistletoe Inn."

"It's my first time in Vermont."

"Why did you choose *this* writers' conference?"

"It sounded like a good one. But, honestly, mostly because H. T. Cowell is going to be here. I wanted to hear him speak."

"That's a lot of money to hear someone speak."

"He's worth it," I said. "He's the reason I decided to be a writer. I can't believe that he's really going to be here in person."

"Isn't he a bit of a recluse?" Samantha asked.

"That's putting it mildly," I said. "He makes J. D. Salinger look like an extrovert. The funny thing is, how do we really even know that the person who speaks is Cowell? I mean, who really knows what he looks like? They could bring in an imposter and no one would even know."

"Maybe the whole Cowell thing was a fraud from the beginning," Samantha said. "And the organizers are just betting that Cowell's too reclusive to ever find out."

Zeke looked amused by our ramblings. "So Cowell's your inspiration?"

I nodded. "He's amazing. I've read some of his books five or six times. How about you?"

"I've read his books," Zeke said. "Not five or six times, but I mostly liked them."

"I just want to know why he stopped writing," I said. "His disappearance from the writing world is one of those great mysteries, like, whatever happened to the Mayans or who was Carly Simon really singing about in 'You're So Vain.' "

"Mick Jagger," Samantha said. "Everyone knows it's Jagger." She looked at me. "It was Jagger, right?"

"I have no idea," I said.

"Maybe the words just stopped coming," Zeke said. "Or maybe he was just old. It's like you said, no one knows much about him. For all we know he's ninety years old."

The idea of him being an old man made me a little sad. "Maybe."

"I don't think it's such a mystery," Samantha said. "I mean, why wouldn't he quit? He sold tens of millions of books, which means he made tens of millions of dollars. If I had his money, I wouldn't keep writing. I'd take the money and move to Bali or the south of France and enjoy life." She looked at Zeke. "Or Florida."

"Maybe it wasn't the money," I said, ignoring her flirtation, "but the pressure to keep succeeding. Like Margaret Mitchell. She hit the top, then just stopped. I mean, after *Gone With the Wind*, where do you go but down?"

"Actually," Zeke said, "Margaret Mitchell claimed that she stopped writing because she was too busy answering fan mail. But it was probably more likely that she just hated the fame and was annoyed by all the people who wouldn't leave her alone. Once she got so mad at a fan who came to her house that she swore that she'd never write another word." Zeke frowned. "Then she was hit by a drunk driver."

"Margaret Mitchell was hit by a drunk driver?" I said.

"That's how she died," Zeke said. "The drunk was a taxi driver with twenty-three previous traffic violations."

"Wasn't Stephen King also hit by a drunk driver?" Samantha asked.

"He was hit by a car, but the driver wasn't drunk. But he did have a lot of traffic violations."

"I heard that the guy who hit him died on Stephen King's birthday," Samantha said.

"That may be true," Zeke said.

"That's creepy," Samantha replied. "Like his books."

"I don't know why Cowell stopped writing," I said. "And maybe we'll never *really* know. But what I do know is that he may be the only man on the planet who understands how a woman feels. I couldn't believe that a man could write like that. For a while I wondered if his books were really written by a woman using a man's name."

"Wait," Samantha said. "That would explain why he hides from the press—or should I say why *she* hides from the press. And why she uses her initials instead of a name that would reveal her true gender, the way Nora Roberts does when she writes her thrillers. H. T. could stand

152

for Helen Taylor. Or maybe it's not just one woman but a group of women."

Zeke nodded. "I used to think that about R. L. Stine, the guy who wrote the Goosebumps books."

"That he was a woman?" Samantha said.

"No, that he was really a group of writers. I mean, he was releasing a new book just about every month and his name is Stine, like Frankenstein. It sounds like a brand, right? Just like Betty Crocker."

Samantha looked confused. "Betty Crocker's not a real person?"

Zeke and I glanced at each other.

"No, Betty Crocker is a fabrication," Zeke said. "Like the Easter bunny. Or the queen of England."

I forced myself not to laugh. Zeke was clearly having fun with her now. Samantha just looked confused.

"And R. L. Stine isn't a real person either," she said.

"No, actually he is," Zeke said. "I met him."

"You met R. L. Stine?" I asked.

"Robert Lawrence Stine," Zeke said. "He goes by Bob. He's a great guy. He started writing humor books for kids under the pen name Jovial Bob Stine, then moved on to kids' horror. He's the man who got millions of boys to read."

"None of this explains why Cowell is such a recluse," Samantha said.

"Maybe he's just so ugly that his publisher

decided to hide him from the public so he didn't ruin women's romantic fantasies."

I shook my head. "You're brutal. And if he does end up coming, I hope you don't meet him. You'll probably just offend him."

"What do you mean, *if* he ends up coming?"

"Last night these women were telling us that he has a habit of missing events he's scheduled for."

Zeke shook his head. "That's the first I've heard of that. What a cad."

I looked at him. "Did you just call him a *cad?*"

"No."

"Yes you did."

"Is that even a word?" Samantha asked.

"It's a word," Zeke said. "Archaic, but still wieldable."

"No one says *cad* anymore," I said.

"You're wrong, because I just did."

"So you admit it."

"I admit it," he said. "Anyone, no matter how famous, who commits to an important event, then, barring some major emergency, doesn't show up, is a *cad*."

"Yeah, you probably shouldn't meet him," Samantha said. "He probably won't like being called a cad, whatever that is."

"It would never happen," Zeke said. "Because if he does show up, he's not a cad."

"He has a point," Samantha said.

"I think you're just jealous," I said.

Zeke thought for a moment, then said, "You're right, of course. We always throw stones upward, don't we?" He turned to me. "It's easy to see why I *wouldn't* like him; men are always jealous of the other rooster in the coop. But the real question is, why do you like him so much? You were a loyal reader and he deserted you, along with millions of others."

"It's his life," I said. "It's not like he owed me anything. And his books helped me during a difficult time of my life." I nodded slowly. "I look forward to seeing him. I just hope I'm not too disappointed."

"I hope not too," Zeke said. "I'd hate to see you waste all that money."

"That would stink," Samantha said.

"I'm also hoping that I might get the chance of getting him to sign something for me."

"What is that?" Zeke asked.

"A first-edition copy of *The Tuscan Promise*."

"You have one of those?"

I nodded. "I was one of the early readers. There were only five thousand of the first editions printed. I bought it for, like, fifteen dollars at the bookstore, but I saw a copy on eBay going for around nine thousand."

"Nine thousand!" he said. "That's insane."

"That's what it was going for."

"You should sell it," he said.

"I'm not going to sell it. To me it's worth more than the money."

"You are a true fan," Zeke said. "And for that reason alone I hope he shows." He turned to Samantha. "What about you, Samantha? What brought you here?"

"A little of everything. Romance, Vermont in the winter, the energy of a writers' conference. But, mostly, Walt was driving me crazy. Frankly I would have gone to a basket-weaving class in Chernobyl to get away from him."

"Who's Walt?" Zeke asked.

"No one," she said, unconsciously leaning toward Zeke.

"He's her fiancé," I said.

Samantha frowned at me.

"How is a fiancé 'no one'?" Zeke asked.

"It's complicated," Samantha said.

"Not really," I said.

"No, not really," she agreed.

Zeke smiled as he poked a fork into his lasagna, which I'm sure was cold by then. He took a bite, then asked me, "What's the rest of your day like?"

"Right after lunch I need to turn in my papers for the agent sessions on Thursday. The sign-up sheet in our packet said our introduction forms and manuscripts are due before one if we want the agents to review them."

"I already turned mine in," Samantha said.

"Did you sign up for an agent?" I asked Zeke.

"No. Not this time," he said. "After you sign up, are you going to any more sessions?"

"I'm going to the Living the Dream presentation."

Samantha said, "Isn't that the one by the guy who was calling himself John Grisham and hitting on us?"

"Yes, unfortunately."

"Why are you going to that? He's a creep."

"Yes, but he's a *published* creep," I said. "So, as far as the afternoon sessions, it's either Faux Grisham, Writing Paranormal Romance, or Exciting Punctuation, and I don't want to spend an hour learning about periods."

"I hate periods," Samantha said.

Zeke squinted. "What?"

"That's not what—" I stopped, too exasperated to explain. "Okay. Punctuation's out. And I don't care for the vampire-love-triangle stuff, so we're back to creepy John Grisham wannabe."

"Well, I better come with you," Samantha said.

I looked at Zeke. "Do you want to come? I don't think he'll hit on you."

"Thank you, but no. I've got some phone calls to catch up on. When should we talk about your book?"

"What about *your* book?" I said.

"I'm not sure it can be saved," he said. "How about we meet for dinner in the dining room at . . . seven."

"Seven is perfect," I said.

He turned to Samantha. "Should I make reservations for three?"

"No," Samantha said, looking disappointed. "I promised my freaky writing buddy that I'd have dinner with her."

"Then it's dinner for two at seven," Zeke said to me. "Don't forget your manuscript. I'll meet you in the lobby."

"I'll see you then."

He got up and left. After he was gone, Samantha said, "Wow, you're totally into him."

"What makes you think that?"

Samantha shook her head. "Because if your smile was any bigger, the top of your head would fall off."

"Okay, I think he's gorgeous and very nice." I frowned. "I hope I'm not that obvious."

"You are," she said. "It's a good thing he likes you too."

"Why do you say that?"

"He was here, right? And he just asked you to dinner? Really, do you need a weatherman to tell you which way the wind blows?"

"Bob Dylan," I said. "You really think he's interested in me?"

Samantha shook her head. "You think? How can a romance writer be so blind to romance?"

"I don't know. I do better in fiction than in real life." I sighed. "All right, let's go. We don't want to keep John Grisham waiting."

Chapter
Sixteen

Some people thrill ride on the road of others' failed journeys.

Kimberly Rossi's Diary

Bready's talk should have been titled: *Narcissism: How So Little Success Can Swell a Head.*

Like everyone else at the retreat, I was hoping to hear an inspirational talk about how someone like me could break into the publishing world. Instead Bready basically made it sound like I'd be better off buying a lottery ticket and praying for success. Actually, he almost used those exact words. He said, "To keep your expectations in perspective, submit your manuscript to a publisher, then buy a lottery ticket. Your chances of winning the lottery are better."

He then went on to attribute his own immeasurable success not to luck but to perseverance, hard work, and remarkable talent. (Surprisingl he left off charm and humility.) Seriously, it was like he was using the same message he had used flirting with me, except this time with a room of eighty people, many of whom were growing visibly annoyed with his hubris. A few walked out before he was done.

A useful, but discouraging, thing I learned from his presentation was that finding a publisher was only the beginning of the process. "Getting published is like qualifying for the Olympics," he said. "You still need to compete, and only a handful of the competitors bring home medals."

Halfway through his speech he rediscovered Samantha and me in the audience and began focusing his remarks almost exclusively on us. It was agonizing. I've never been happier to see an hour pass, and as soon as he finished we hurried out of the session before he could trap us.

After we were outside the room, Samantha said, "If ego were money, that guy could pay off third-world debt."

I laughed. "I'm sorry I dragged you to that. We should have gone to the punctuation class."

"I'm not," she said. "It was informative. I learned a lot."

I looked at her doubtfully. "Really? What did you learn?"

"How some people live to sap the hope out of dreamers. It's like once they reach the top, they cut the rope."

"You may be right," I said. "Though I wouldn't say he's reached the top."

"As high as he's going to get," Samantha said. "So where to now?"

"You choose the next session," I said. I took out my conference schedule. "We have three choices. *E-lectric: How to Heat Up the Internet with Your e-Book.*"

"That sounds important."

"*Making a Six-Figure Salary on Four-Figure*

Book Sales: How to Make a Lucrative Living as a Midlist Author."

"That sounds boring."

"And *Chopping the Writer's Block: How to Keep Writing When the Words Stop Coming.*"

"That sounds like something I need," Samantha said.

"I was thinking the same thing. Let's go learn how to chop some writer's block."

Chapter
Seventeen

Zeke and I had dinner tonight.
I swear I know him from somewhere.

Kimberly Rossi's Diary

The main message of the writer's block lecture was that there is no universal cure for writer's block and you have to figure out for yourself what works for you—which made me think there was no reason to go to the class.

I did learn one thing of value. Walking sometimes helps. Thoreau believed that our legs are connected to our brains. I vowed to walk more.

After the conference I went back to my room to rest a little before dinner. I lay on my bed for a few minutes, then rolled over and looked at my manuscript. "*The Mistletoe Promise*," I said. "By Kimberly Rossi. *New York Times* bestselling author." I groaned. *Right*. I wondered if Zeke would hate my book.

A few minutes before seven I freshened up my hair and makeup, grabbed my manuscript, and walked out to the lobby. Zeke was waiting for me, sitting on one of the crushed-velvet chairs, somehow looking even more beautiful than he had at noon. He stood as I entered. "Hi."

"Hi," I said, walking up to him.

"How were the rest of your sessions? Did you learn anything?"

"I learned that Bready guy is a *cad*."

Zeke smiled. "See, it's a useful word that bears repetition."

The dining room was crowded with a long line of people waiting for a table. The hostess smiled at us as we walked in. "Good evening, Mr. Faulkner. Right this way."

Zeke had reserved a small table for us by a window near the back of the room. The table was set with crystal and a flickering candle. He pulled my chair back for me, which, sadly, threw me a little. Apart from my father, I wasn't used to being with a gentleman.

"I hear the tourtière is very good." He looked up at me. "You're not vegetarian, are you?"

"No. What's tourtière?"

"It's a Canadian meat pie that's made with diced pork, veal, or beef. The chef here told me that he adds venison to it to enhance the flavor."

"That sounds interesting," I said. "Not interesting enough to actually order, but interesting."

He smiled. "Vermont has some interesting food. Bonne Bouche cheese, Dilly beans, fiddlehead ferns, Anadama bread."

"I have no idea what any of those things are."

"Neither do I, and I've eaten all of them. But you can't go wrong with Vermont dairy products. Especially their cheese."

"I love cheese," I said.

We shared some cheese with a duck sausage and cornmeal polenta appetizer, then Zeke ordered a bottle of wine. For my entrée I ordered the goat's milk gnocchi with tomato and pine nuts, while Zeke had the Gloucester cod. After we ordered, Zeke said, "Tell me about yourself."

"What would you like to know?"

"Let's start from the beginning. Have you always lived in Colorado?"

"No, I was raised in Las Vegas."

"Vegas. So you're good with cards?"

"No. I don't gamble." Then I added, "At least not with money."

"What took you to Colorado?"

"My ex, Marcus. He got a job offer in Boulder."

"What did Marcus do?"

"He was a history professor. Now he's just history."

Zeke smiled. "That sounds like a country song. So things didn't work out."

"The *Titanic* didn't work out. My marriage was a disaster."

He chuckled.

"You want the story?"

"I love a good anecdote," he said. "If you're willing to share."

"Why not?" I said. "Marcus and I had been not-so-happily married for about three years when he got the job offer in Colorado. I thought it would be good for our relationship, but two years after we moved, he was caught in a campus sting operation. Apparently he was 'romantically'

166

involved with several of his students, trading grades for . . . *favors.*"

"Adds a whole new meaning to *extracurricular activity,*" Zeke said with a bemused expression. Then he said, "I'm sorry, I shouldn't joke about that. It's pretty horrific."

"It was horrific."

His brow furrowed. "Did that story make national news?"

"I'm afraid so."

"I think I read about it. I'm sorry."

"And, to add insult to painful injury, after everything hit, he left me for one of his students. Actually, two of his students. So I'm the one who ended up alone."

Zeke shook his head. "That's truly horrific."

"Samantha thinks it's good fodder for a romance."

"More like fodder for a horror story," Zeke said.

"That's what I said. Especially when you add the prologue about my two unsuccessful engagements before Marcus. One left me at the altar, the other got signed by the Orlando Magic and ended our engagement with a text message."

"Classy," Zeke said. "Would I know the player?"

I remembered that Zeke lived in Florida. "You might. Danny Iverson."

Zeke shook his head. "Sorry."

167

"It was a while back," I said. "He only lasted two seasons before his career fizzled."

"That's karma," Zeke said.

I looked at him for a moment. "With my record, it probably seems weird to you that I want to be a romance writer."

"Not at all. It makes perfect sense."

"It does?"

"Absolutely. It's like this. I have two brothers, Matthias and Dominic. When they were young they both wanted to play the piano. Even though Matthias was older, Dominic was naturally gifted and could play by ear.

"Once we were sitting around listening to the radio when a new Billy Joel song came on. It was 'Vienna' from the *Stranger* album. After it played Matthias said, 'I wonder if they have sheet music for that.'

"Dominic walked over to the piano and played the song flawlessly. I've never once heard him practice. He never had to.

"Matthias was the opposite. He'd get up an hour before the rest of us every morning to practice piano. Most of the time it was agonizing listening to him, since he usually couldn't go more than thirty seconds without hitting the wrong key. But he never gave up. He'd sit there day after day pounding away like he was chiseling a statue.

"Even though he never got as good as Dominic, Dominic eventually lost interest and stopped playing. Matthias is now teaching music at a university and plays for a large Methodist church on Sundays." Zeke looked intensely into my eyes. "I understand why you want to write. We don't appreciate the things that come easy to us as much as we do the things we have to work for. I think that's true for love as well."

No one, including me, had ever understood my dream. I was at a loss for words. After a moment I asked, "What about you? Have you ever been married?"

His expression fell. "I was. For seven years."

"Was," I said. "That sounds ominous. What happened?"

"She left me."

"Why?"

"Now there's a question," he said.

"You'd take her back if you could?"

"That's not an option, but yes, I would."

I sensed that he didn't want to talk about it. "I'm sorry."

"Life happens," he said. He took a deep breath, then looked back at me. "So, back to you. Do you have siblings?"

"No. I was an only child."

"And your parents are still in Vegas?"

"My father is. My mother died when I was young."

"How did she die?"

I lied. "She had breast cancer."

"I'm sorry," he said. "How old were you when she died?"

"I was eleven."

"I'm really sorry," he said. "Are you close to your father?"

"He's my best friend." To my surprise, my eyes began to well up. "I'm sorry. He has cancer."

"I'm sorry he has cancer," Zeke said. "That must be especially hard since you already lost your mother to it."

I didn't reply.

"What kind of cancer does he have?"

"Colon cancer."

"What stage is it in?"

"Three A."

He nodded slightly. "Then his odds are still good."

I was surprised that he knew that. "That's what he said."

"Does he have good care?"

I shook my head. "It's been an issue between us. He's a Vietnam veteran, so he goes to the VA hospital. I don't think the care is that good. He needs surgery and chemo, but they won't even get him in until next February."

"Why are they waiting so long?"

"That's what I asked him, but he just shrugged it off with 'it's just how it is.' What makes it worse is that Las Vegas has one of the top cancer institutes in the country."

"The Henderson Clinic," Zeke said.

I looked at him. "How did you know that?"

"Years ago I did some business with them," he said. "It's a state-of-the-art facility. They have one of the highest recovery rates in the world."

I nodded. "That's what I heard. I wish he'd go there. But he never would."

"Why not?"

"He'd never spend the money. He'd rather die and leave what money he has to me." I suddenly felt angry. "He's so stubborn. He paid for this whole conference up front, then told me I had to go. He said he'd be disappointed in me if I didn't go."

"And his disappointment matters to you?"

"Yes, it matters. He's lived his whole life for me. He's my hero."

To my surprise, Zeke suddenly looked moved as well. "Why was it so important to him that you came?"

"He knows it's my dream to be a writer, so he wants that for me. But now I think I want it more for him."

"I can see why he's your hero," Zeke said. He thoughtfully took a sip of wine. After he set his glass back down he asked, "Does he think he's going to die?"

I thought it a peculiar question. "No."

"Then he probably won't."

"Why do you say that?"

171

"It's just a theory, but I think we know our time. Maybe it's more cause than effect, but I think we have a sense of when we're going to die. Not always, of course. But sometimes. I've heard at least a dozen stories of people who spontaneously put their affairs in order before dying unexpectedly, like in a car accident."

I pondered the assertion. "With him, I don't know," I said. "He's a war vet. He thinks he's indestructible."

Zeke shook his head. "None of the war vets I know think they're indestructible. Not after what they've seen."

Again I was filled with emotion and I dabbed my eyes with my napkin. "May we talk about something else?"

"Of course," he said. "I'm sorry."

"It's okay. Thank you for asking about him."

For a moment we sat in silence. Then he asked, "When did you know you wanted to be a writer?"

"I was barely twenty. I wasn't exaggerating when I said it was Cowell who made me want to write. It was one of those really hard times in my life. My first engagement had fallen through a month earlier when I came across *The Tuscan Promise*. It was the first book of Cowell's I read. It was also the first time a book really made me feel loved. I didn't know how that was possible. I thought, this is like spiritual alchemy, turning ink into emotion. It was the closest thing I could imagine to magic. I wanted to be a magician like that."

Zeke looked at me thoughtfully. "That was the most beautiful reason I've ever heard for someone wanting to be a writer. You have a poet's heart."

"Thank you," I said. "Have you read that book?"

He nodded. "It was a long time ago. Honestly, I don't remember much about it."

"I mostly remember how I felt when I read it." I breathed out. "What about you? When did you know you wanted to be a writer?"

"I was fourteen and the book was *The Hobbit*. It was the first time that a book had transported me to a different world. More than anything I wanted to write fantasy, so I started writing every day. Today we'd call it fan fiction, but I wrote about the world Tolkien had created with orcs and hobbits and trolls. I was a total nerd. Then, two years later, I fell in love for the first time and that changed everything." He grinned. "It was like a child's first taste of sugar. I've had a sweet tooth ever since."

Just then the waiter brought out our meals. After we had both started eating I said, "What was her name? Your first love."

He smiled shyly and I thought he looked cute. "Linda Nash," he said almost reverently. "She had long blond hair, Windex-blue eyes, and go-go boots."

"Go-go boots?"

"Go-go boots." He laughed and shook his head. "Man, I was smitten. I had never felt that kind of angst before, like pain and ecstasy in the same breath. She'd look at me and my mind would go blank."

"Did she like you back?"

He shook his head. "I have no idea. I was a kid. I never even told her how I felt. Her father was a salesman and her family moved away the next year. But the damage was done. Falling in love was transformative, because that's when I realized that all stories, at their core, are love stories. Whether you're talking about *Star Wars* or *East of Eden.*

"At first I went a little overboard and just wrote love letters, sonnets, poems, syrupy stuff— things that would never be published, but I wrote for the joy of writing. And I fell in love with falling in love."

"Most men aren't like that."

"Probably more than you think," he said. "They just don't use women's language to express it."

"I've never thought of it that way," I said. "So that's why you wanted to write romance?"

"Maybe," he said.

"Maybe?"

"At one of these conferences an author told me that when he was sixteen he was walking through a mall when he saw a man signing books for a long line of women and it occurred to him that if you want to get a girl, there was no better way than being a writer of romance. Smart man, I thought. Where else would women looking for romance line up to meet you? Of course musicians figured this out millennia ago."

"So is that really why you want to be a writer? To meet women?"

He looked at me with a hint of a smile. "On some deep, primal level—much deeper than I'd be willing to admit—that's probably true. I think Freud would argue that's true of all male endeavors."

"Men are pathetic," I said.

"And women wear high heels, why?"

"To play off men's pathetic nature."

"So who's more pathetic, the junkie or the dealer?"

"That's the question, isn't it?" I said.

"Indeed," he replied. He looked me in the eyes. "I will admit that I'm very glad that I met you."

"I'm glad I met you too."

After a moment he said, "So back to your original question, why do I want to be a writer? Primal urges aside, I started writing because I'm not cutthroat enough to run a Fortune 500 company, I'm not handsome enough to be an actor or model, I can't sing, and I'm not coordinated enough to be a professional athlete.

But I did win a tenth-grade creative-writing contest, so I went with my strength."

"I disagree with you on the handsome part. You're definitely handsome enough to be an actor or a model."

"You're being kind."

"I'm being honest. The first time I saw you I thought, That guy is gorgeous."

"Was that before or after you fell off the treadmill and hit your head?"

"I didn't hit my head, and it was before that. And thank you for reminding me that your first impression of me was that I'm a klutz."

"I just thought you were flirting with me."

"By almost killing myself? Really?"

"Any romance writer knows that showing vulnerability is a powerful lure. In the old days a woman would drop her handkerchief. You dropped a towel."

"I dropped my whole body."

"Even better," he said. "It's the whole politically incorrect damsel-in-distress thing."

I just laughed. "So after you decided to be a writer, then what?"

"I got an English degree and taught high school English for six years before I got into real estate."

"And you like real estate?"

He shrugged. "It pays the bills better than teaching did."

We ate awhile in silence, then he said, "So, moment of truth. May I see your book?"

I had actually forgotten that I had brought my manuscript with me. I leaned over and picked it up from the floor. "I can't believe I'm sharing it. When do I get to read yours?"

"Soon," he said. He took the manuscript and immediately started reading.

"Don't read it now," I said. "I'll be embarrassed."

He looked up. "Has anyone read this yet?"

"Other than my father and the publishers that rejected it, you're the first one."

"It's an honor," he said. "I promise that I'll be gentle with my critique and effusive with my praise."

"I just want to know if it's any good," I said. "Or if I should stop writing."

"Those two things have nothing to do with each other," he said. "If you enjoy writing, you should write, whether anyone else likes it or not." He looked back down at the manuscript. "*The Mistletoe Promise*. Did you name it after this conference?"

"No. It's a coincidence. I named it that more than two years ago. What do you think of it?"

"I think it's an intriguing title." He set my manuscript aside. "Would you care for dessert?"

"Not tonight," I said.

He took a sip of wine, then said, "I'm eager to start reading your book. Shall we go?"

Zeke paid the bill, then we walked out to the lobby. "What floor is your room on?"

"This floor. It's right down that hall."

"May I walk you to your room?"

"Yes, thank you."

We walked down the short hallway, stopping at my doorway. "You're really in room 101?"

"Yes. Why?"

"It's Orwellian," he said. "And strangely ironic. In Orwell's book *1984*, Room 101 is the torture room in the Ministry of Love, where people face their greatest fear."

"They're tortured in the Ministry of Love?"

"It's newspeak," he said. "Kind of like American society today. Did you read the book?"

"In middle school, but apparently I've forgotten it." As I took out my card key I said, "And I am facing one of my greatest fears. I just hope you don't hate my book."

"I'm not going to hate your book," he said.

"How do you know?"

"I read the first paragraph."

"You can tell if a book's good by the first paragraph?"

"No. But I can tell if a writer's good by the first paragraph."

I cocked my head. "You're acting very confident for an unpublished author."

He smiled. "You don't have to be a chef to know if the food's good."

"Touché," I said.

"I'll make you two promises. First, I promise that I will withhold all judgment until I've read the entire book. Second, I promise that I will be completely honest with you."

"Thank you," I said. "I think." I pondered what he'd said a moment, then added, "I'm not sure that I want that."

"Trust me, you do," he said. "And remember, I also promised to be gentle."

"I'll hold you to that."

He looked into my eyes, then said softly, "Thank you for having dinner with me. You're very lovely."

I suddenly felt a little flustered. "Thank you. So did you."

A large smile spread across his face. "I better go. I might be up all night reading." There was an awkward pause, and I hoped that he would kiss me. Instead he put out his hand. "Good night."

I took his hand trying not to show my disappointment. "Good night. I'll see you tomorrow."

With my manuscript in his hands, he turned and walked away. I went inside my room and lay down on my bed. *You're very lovely. Thank you. So did you? That doesn't make any sense.* Then I said out loud, "Please like me anyway." I couldn't believe that I had only met him that morning. I remembered a line I had read in one of Cowell's books: *Love takes shortcuts.* It certainly had. Then I had a strange thought. *Is there really such a thing as a soul mate? If not, why do I feel like I've met him before?*

Chapter
Eighteen

*I feel like I've stepped
over the edge of a cliff.*

Kimberly Rossi's Diary

The next morning Zeke wasn't in the fitness center and I wondered if he had really stayed up reading my book. My fears started in on me. What if he hated my book and was now avoiding me? I shook my head. *Why do I always torture myself with the worst possible outcome?*

Coming back from the fitness center, I stopped in the dining room. I was running late and Samantha wasn't there, so I grabbed a banana and yogurt and took it back to my room to get ready for the day. An hour later I walked into the workshop anticipating seeing Zeke, but he wasn't there either. He still hadn't arrived when our facilitator started the meeting.

"Let's see, who are we missing?" Karen asked, looking at her list. "Zeke is AWOL. Who is Zeke's writing buddy?"

Almost everyone looked at me.

"I am," I said, slightly raising my hand. "But I haven't seen him this morning."

"Today we're sharing, so you'll need to pair up with another group," she said.

"You can come with us," Heather said.

I tried to look grateful for the invitation. "Thanks."

I had nothing to share. I had only brought three copies of my book, two for the agents and now

Zeke had my third, so I spent the entire workshop listening to Heather and her writing buddy, an eighty-year-old woman, read chapter after chapter of the most cloying love stories ever penned and feigning interest. I was glad when the workshop was over.

As I walked out of the room Samantha was waiting for me, her face twisted with disgust. "I can't even begin to tell you how much I hate my workshop group. I swear they're all freaks."

"And why is this?"

"They spent the whole session arguing over who kisses better, a vampire or a werewolf. What they finally decided was that a vampire is good with its mouth and sucking, where the werewolf is in touch with its inner animal." She breathed out. "What do you think?"

I tried not to smile. "I think it comes down to whether you like hairy men or smooth ones."

"Good point," she said. "I should have said that. Walter isn't hairy at all. Like, my writing buddy is hairier than he is."

"Isn't your writing buddy a woman?"

"That's my point," she said. "I missed you at breakfast this morning."

"Sorry. I was running late so I just grabbed something and took it to my room."

"I thought maybe you'd run off with Clooney."

"No. I don't even know where he is today. He skipped the workshop."

"He wasn't in your workshop?"

"No."

"But you did have dinner last night?"

"Yes."

"And how did that go?"

"It was nice."

"By 'nice' do you mean Walmart greeter nice or Brad Pitt nice?"

"What are you asking?"

"I'll spell it out. Are. You. In. Love?"

I stared at her. "I just met him yesterday."

"And your point is . . ."

"My point is, I just met him yesterday."

She shook her head. "Seriously, you're a romance writer. If you don't believe in love at first sight, you might as well turn in your pen. Did you give him your book?"

"Yes."

She smiled triumphantly. "I knew it."

"You knew what? He's my workshop partner. I was supposed to give it to him."

"Giving him your book is like standing naked in front of him."

"I didn't stand naked in front of him."

"That's your problem."

I shook my head. "You're going to drive me crazy," I said. "Let's go. There's a session on the roles of men and women in modern romance."

"Yeah, you should definitely go to that one," she said.

•••

In spite of my denial, Samantha was right on two accounts. First, she'd detected that giddy, butterflies-in-the-stomach feeling I couldn't shake. Second, what Samantha had said about sharing my book was true. I felt naked and vulnerable and afraid. I wished I hadn't given it to him. I wasn't looking forward to his critique.

Chapter
Nineteen

Today's lecture on gender roles reminded me of a quote from Camille Paglia: "Woman is the dominant sex. Men have to do all sorts of stuff to prove that they are worthy of woman's attention." I wish I found that more true in my life.

Kimberly Rossi's Diary

The session on gender roles in modern romance was more interesting than I thought it would be. The presenter challenged the notion that a romance novel should be about helpless women and dominating men. Instead she proposed that in the true romance, it is the female who subjugates and tames the male by exposing his vulnerabilities. She quoted romance novelist Jayne Ann Krentz as saying, "the woman always wins. With courage, intelligence, and gentleness she brings the most dangerous creature on earth, the human male, to his knees."

I wished that had happened in my real life. It seemed like I was always the one who ended up broken.

Samantha and I had lunch together, then I went back to my room to rest a little before the next session. I noticed that the message light on my phone was flashing.

"Kim, it's Zeke. Sorry I missed you. If you don't have plans, I'd love to get together again for dinner. You can call my room, it's number . . ." He hesitated. "Actually, I don't know if this room has a number. Just call the hotel operator and ask for me. Bye."

I pushed zero on the phone. The operator

answered. "How may I help you, Ms. Rossi?"

"Could you please connect me with Mr. Zeke Faulkner?"

"Do you know what room number that is?"

"No, sorry."

"Just a moment, please." There was a long pause. "Here you go. Have a good day."

Zeke answered on the third ring. "Hello."

"Zeke? It's Kim."

"Good, you got my message. Thank you for calling."

"Of course," I said. "I'd love to go to dinner again."

"Excellent," he replied.

"I missed you in workshop today. Busy with work?"

"No, I was in my room reading your book."

"Really?"

"I told you that I would. I'm just about finished. So what are you doing before dinner?"

"Samantha and I are going to the Catherine McCullin speech."

"I saw that she's here. Mind if I tag along?"

"Of course not. I'll meet you in the lobby."

Catherine McCullin's presentation was the final session of the afternoon. I met Samantha standing outside the ballroom. "I saved us seats," she said.

"Zeke's joining us," I said. "So we'll need one extra."

"You found Clooney?"

"He called," I said.

"Good, and no problem with the seats. I already saved us three."

"Why did you save three?"

"I didn't want anyone sitting next to me," she replied. "But I'm okay with Clooney."

"Why don't you go ahead and sit down and I'll wait for Zeke," I said.

"All right. We're in the front row, left of center."

"How do you get such good seats?"

"I'm aggressive," she said, walking to the ballroom.

Less than a minute later, Zeke walked out of the elevator. He smiled when he saw me. "Hey, beautiful." He kissed me on the cheek. "Thank you for letting me join you."

"I'm glad you are. Samantha's already inside with our seats." I desperately wanted to ask him if he'd finished my book but decided to wait for him to bring it up.

As we walked together into the ballroom I asked, "Have you ever read one of McCullin's books?"

Zeke shook his head. "No. Fictionalized Hollywood gossip isn't really my thing. I'm not interested in the real stuff, why would I want a fictionalized version? How about you?"

"I'm the same. I've only read one of her books. It was my first and last."

We found Samantha in the front of the room and sat down.

"Did you know McCullin has sold more than a hundred million books?" Samantha said to us. "I want to be her."

"Be careful of what you wish for," Zeke said softly.

Everyone went wild when McCullin came out onstage. Her speech was titled *The Limousine Lifestyle of the Bestselling Author* and consisted mostly of name-dropping and celebrity gossip until the end of her talk, when she focused on personal spending sprees that included a $10,000 laser haircut, a $218,000 pair of high-heeled shoes with thirty carats of diamonds, and a very long story about the time she made her pool boy fill her hot tub with Perrier because she liked the feel of its "effervescence on her skin."

"It took more than two thousand of those quart bottles," she said. "He drained every 7-Eleven, Safeway, and Walmart between Beverly Hills and Burbank."

Everyone in the audience seemed amused by McCullin's anecdotes. I was bothered by them. Successful or not, she wasted more than six thousand dollars on soaking in tingly water while my father, who had worked hard his whole life, couldn't get the health care he needed. The more she went on with her stories the more I wanted to walk out of the session. I glanced over at Zeke. He didn't look happy either.

After her speech was over the house lights went up while McCullin was still on the stage, thronged by the local press as well as conference attendees wanting her autograph.

"That was something," Zeke said dully. I nodded in agreement.

As we were crossing in front of the stage, McCullin suddenly turned toward us and shouted, "Zeke, baby. Call me."

Zeke gave her a short wave but continued on with the flow of the crowd. I looked at him with amazement. When we got outside I said, "You know her?"

"The impressive thing," Samantha said, "is that *she* knows *him*."

Zeke looked uncomfortable. "Not really; we met at a writers' conference a while back." He looked at me. "It's nothing."

I was still a bit stunned. "You met at a writers' conference and she remembers you?"

"So, I'm unforgettable."

"Did you see her diamond ring?" Samantha asked. "It covered like three knuckles. I don't know how she could lift her hand with that rock on." She turned to Zeke. "Would you introduce me to her?"

"I'd rather not," he replied. "She's not exactly . . . cordial."

"She seemed cordial to you," Samantha said.

"He means to the little people," I said.

Samantha frowned.

"So, what did Mr. Unforgettable think of her presentation?" I asked.

Zeke scratched his head. "She's an entertaining speaker, but I'm not a fan of conscienceless excess. There are millions of people in this world who can't find healthy drinking water, and she's joking about bathing in Perrier."

I was glad that he felt the same way that I did. "I know, right? And $200,000 shoes? I'd pay my father's hospital bills. And others'."

"I know you would," he said.

"Do you think she really did those things?" Samantha asked.

Zeke nodded. "Yes. I'm sure she did."

I excused myself and went back to my room to freshen up, then met Zeke in the waiting area of the hotel's dining room. Again we didn't have to wait to get a table. In fact, we sat at the exact same table as the night before.

"Why don't we have to wait like everyone else?" I asked.

"I tipped the hostess," he said. "They must not get paid much."

"I'm not complaining," I said.

As he pulled out my chair for me, I said, "I'm still a little shocked that Catherine McCullin knows you."

"I'm sure she knows a lot of people."

"But she asked you to call her, which means she thinks you have her phone number." I looked at him. "Do you?"

"You're not going to let up on this, are you?" he asked.

I shook my head.

"We had dinner once. But, like you said about her books, first and last time."

"I'm impressed. There's a lot more to you than meets the eye."

"That's true of everyone," he said. "There's always more to the book than the cover. Even a bad book."

"Are you a bad book?" I asked flippantly.

To my surprise he turned serious. "There are better books on the shelf." He lifted his menu. "Now what will you be having?"

A few minutes later, the waiter came and took our orders. I ordered a salmon salad and Zeke ordered the prime rib with sweet potatoes.

After the waiter left I leaned forward in my seat. "So what do you think of my book?"

"I'm still reading it."

"But what do you think of it so far?"

"I'm not going to tell you until I read the final word. You wouldn't judge *A Farewell to Arms* until the last page, would you?"

"If Hemingway asked me what I thought of the first chapter, I'd tell him. Just tell me if you like what you've read so far."

"I'll tell you this. You can definitely write. That's all I'll say for now."

I took a deep breath. "Fair enough." I took a drink of wine. "I had this thought today. There's more than a hundred writers here. There's probably a hundred more of these conferences around the country. I'm guessing that less than one in ten thousand will ever make a living writing, which means our odds are better in Vegas."

"That's not hopeful," Zeke said.

"I'm just being realistic," I said. "So what if what we write is never published?"

Zeke's expression took on an exaggerated gravity. "If an author writes a book and it's never published, did the book exist?"

"I'm being serious," I said. "Sometimes I wonder why we bother to write at all."

Zeke looked suddenly thoughtful. "John Updike said, 'We're past the age of heroes and hero kings. . . . Most of our lives are basically mundane and dull, and it's up to the writer to find ways to make them interesting.' " He looked into my eyes. "Writing is life. Sometimes it's all that remains of civilizations.

"Do you know where the oldest writings were found? On tortoise shells. The Chinese carved histories into tortoise shells, then broke them for divination. We know of their wars and strivings from tortoise shells. From their writings. We write, therefore we are."

"I like your brain," I said.

He leaned forward and smiled. "Me too."

A few minutes later our waiter brought out our food, which was again delicious. We ate for a while, then I said, "There's something I've been wondering."

He looked up from his meal. "Yes?"

"Why did you pick me as your partner?"

"I told you. I thought your book sounded interesting."

I was hoping for more. "That's the only reason?"

He looked at me for a moment, then said, "No. When I first saw you in the fitness center I hoped that you were with the romance writers. I wanted to get to know you better. Call it chemistry."

"In school I was good at chemistry."

"Clearly."

"And then we ended up in the same workshop," I said. "That was a nice coincidence."

"It wasn't a coincidence," he said.

"What do you mean?"

"I wasn't supposed to be in group C. I changed because that's where you were."

"But they said that they didn't allow changes."

"I'm sure they don't."

"You mean you lied about Jill sending you to group C?"

"Not really," he said. "I figured that Jill, being

the head of the romance writers, was a staunch proponent of romance, so when I said Jill wanted me in group C, I was telling the truth, in a matter of speaking."

I laughed. "I can't believe you did that."

"Are you glad I did?"

"I'm very glad." I picked at my meal, then said, "So is that what this is? A romance?"

He just smiled.

An hour later we shared an apple crisp dessert. As we finished eating he said, "We better go."

"It's still early."

"I know," he said. "But I need to finish your book."

"I'm flattered that you're really reading it."

"It's an easy read."

I frowned. "Do you mean it's too simple?"

"Good writing *is* simple. Hemingway once wrote, 'If I had more time, I'd write a shorter book.' "

"Then you're saying it's not *too* simple."

"No," he said. "It's not. The scientist who can explain complex theories to the layman is brilliant. Accessibility is true genius."

"I'm definitely accessible," I said.

A large smile crossed his face. "I hope so."

Chapter

Twenty

I suppose, like most people, I don't really want to hear truth; I want to hear good things. If they happen to be true, so much the better.

Kimberly Rossi's Diary

The next morning I had breakfast with Samantha. Outside it was snowing hard—hard enough that some of the hotel guests were stranded and the lobby was crowded with disgruntled travelers and their mounds of luggage.

I didn't see Zeke until our workshop. When I walked in he was sitting next to Karen, talking to her. He smiled when he saw me and motioned to the seat next to him.

"I finished your book," he said. "Every word."

He had a perfect poker face, and I couldn't tell whether he liked or hated it. "And?"

"Let's talk about it tonight."

"You hated it."

"Don't go there," he said. "Are you up for another dinner?"

"I'm always up for dinner."

"If the weather improves, I thought we could go into town. I'm starting to feel a little caged. It would be nice to escape the property for the evening."

"I was thinking the same thing," I said.

I left the last session early. Actually, everyone did. It was titled *From Walmart to Hollywood*, with bestselling author Deborah Mackey. The session was Skyped in, and probably due to the weather, the reception was poor. Finally the facilitator just disconnected the call and apologized for the technical difficulties.

I didn't really care. I was glad for the extra time to get ready for our date. As I entered the lobby, Zeke was already standing near the front door. He again kissed me on the cheek. "You look gorgeous."

"So do you."

"Are you ready to go?" he asked.

"Yes, I'm starving. Where are we going?"

"The concierge recommended a little Italian restaurant in Burlington called L'Amante. Does that sound all right?"

"Sounds perfect," I said.

"Good. My car's outside."

It was still snowing as we walked out of the hotel, though not nearly as hard as it had been earlier. The car Zeke had rented was a Mercedes-Benz four-wheel drive. He opened my door for me and I got in, then he came around and climbed into the driver's seat. "Buckle up," he said. "The roads are still a little slick."

I pulled the seat belt over my chest as he drove off into the winter night.

The restaurant, L'Amante, was about a thirty-five-minute drive from the inn. It reminded me a little of Salvatore's in Vegas.

After we were seated I asked Zeke, "How did you know I liked Italian?"

"You ordered the gnocchi the other night," he said. "And you are Italian. Rossi is an Italian name, right?"

"Yes, it means red."

"I knew that," he said. "I studied Italian when I spent a summer in Florence. I was thinking about moving there permanently. It was right after my wife left me and I needed a clean break. Have you ever been to Italy?"

"No. My father and I have talked about going, but it always seems like something comes up." I looked down at the menu. "What are you getting?"

"The concierge at the hotel recommended the orecchiette if you like eggplant."

"I hate eggplant."

"Avoid the orecchiette," he said.

To start our meal, Zeke ordered an expensive bottle of Chianti, a cheese and salami plate, and an arugula salad with shavings of pecorino cheese, roasted beets, pine nuts, and balsamic vinegar. The moment the waiter left our table I pounced.

"So what did you think of my book?"

"Have some wine," he said.

"It's that bad?"

"I didn't say that." He filled my glass with wine and waited until I took a drink. "All right, my critique. The bottom line is, I've got good news, good news, good news, and a little bad news."

"Let's start with the bad news," I said.

"Why would you want to start with the bad news?"

"It's the way I roll," I said. "Eat the bad stuff first, save dessert for last."

He nodded. "All right. The bad news is, your book's not publishable."

His words hit me like a fist in the stomach. When I could speak I said, "You call that a *little* bad news?"

"It is," he said. "Because the good news is, you've got an ear for dialogue, a great sense of pacing, and you can definitely turn a sentence. In other words, you can write. And that's really good news, because, in the end, you either hear the music or you don't. You hear the music."

I think he expected this to compensate for his rejection, but I was still reeling. He continued.

"The second piece of good news is, you've got a great concept for a book, which is much harder to come by than most people realize. And third, your book is fixable."

I just looked at him, my heart and mind aching.

"Let's go back to the not-publishable part," I said. "What's wrong with it?"

"Okay," he said, looking disappointed that I'd focused on the negative. "There are two problems. First, it's not romance you're writing, it's fantasy."

"You said fantasy *is* romance."

"But I didn't say that romance is fantasy."

"What does that mean?"

"Your people aren't credible."

"What's wrong with my characters?"

"Precisely that," he said. "You're not writing characters. You're writing people. And in the real world, even the best of people are flawed. Your people aren't. And neither is their relationship. Love is full of pain and mistakes. That's what makes it interesting and that's why we explore relationships in literature. That whole 'love is never having to say you're sorry' crap is just that, crap. Love is learning *how* to say you're sorry. It's the trial and error and correction that makes it worthwhile."

I just looked at him.

"Let me put it this way. Love is like learning how to dance. When you first hear the music, you're full of passion and you don't care who's watching because you just want to fling your-self around like an idiot. It's clumsy and it's full of missteps and falls and sometimes you're not even dancing to the same tune, but you don't notice because you're so carried away by the music.

"But then the music begins to wane, and you start stepping on each other's toes. Some think that's the truth of the relationship and run. But the truth is, that's where true love begins. That's when you start to learn each other's rhythm and how to move together. And if you stick with it long enough, you might even learn to be graceful."

After a moment I said, "I guess none of my dance partners stuck around long enough for me to learn that."

"There's that too," he said. "You need to have a partner who cares about the dance. Without that, you won't get far."

I took a deep breath, considering his words. I wasn't even sure how to fix what he'd already suggested. Finally I said, "You said there were two problems."

"The second is tougher," he said.

As if the first wasn't painful enough. My heart already hurt. I dreaded hearing what he had to say.

He looked into my eyes. "Actually, it's a symptom of the same problem. The reason your people aren't believable is because you're not bleeding through them."

"What do you mean?"

"I once heard a writer say, 'It's easy to write a novel; you just slit your wrist and let it bleed on the pages.' She was right. There's not enough of your own blood on these pages. You're not vulner-able enough and you can't hide that. You have pain in your life; let it out in your words. It's like you're writing with gloves on. Take them off. Let the reader really see you. Let them know your fears and hurts. Sophocles and Freud believed that we are defined by our fears. There's a lot of truth to that. When you share your greatest fears, your vulnerability, we bond On that honesty. We connect with each other and we don't feel so alone. And that's what books are really about. Connecting."

Tears began to well up in my eyes. "What if I don't want to share that part of me?"

"Then don't write."

I don't know why hearing this from him hurt so much but it did. I felt humiliated and dumb. I wiped my eyes. "If you know so much, why aren't you published? Why should I listen to you?"

"That's a good question," he said calmly. "Why should you listen to me? Don't. Listen to yourself. You're a writer. So ask yourself if what I'm saying is true. You'll know the answer."

I wiped my eyes with my napkin, avoiding his gaze.

"Kim, when I took your manuscript I promised you that I would be honest. But truthfully, I lied. Because if I thought your writing was beyond saving, I wouldn't have been so direct. I would have told you what you wanted to hear, not what you should hear. But you are a very good writer—good enough to be published. And I believe you have the potential to someday be a great writer. An Amy Tan or a Nora Roberts. But you can't do that halfway."

I took another breath, then quickly dabbed my eyes with my napkin. "May I have some more wine?"

"Of course," he said. He poured my glass Nearly to the brim and I took a sip, then a bigger one, hoping to dull some of the pain I felt.

"We can fix this," he said, holding up my manuscript. "I can help you get this right."

I set down my glass. "We?"

"If you want my help."

"You have your own book to work on," I said.

"It can wait," he replied. "I've waited years for this one, what's another few months?"

I knew that he had meant the offer kindly, but all I could feel was the pain of rejection. After a moment I said, "I don't want your help. May I have my book back, please?"

My response hurt him. "Of course," he said softly, handing me the manuscript. "I'm sorry if what I said came out harsh. I would never intentionally hurt you."

"You have your opinion," I said.

The rest of the evening was miserable. We barely spoke, and I regretted leaving the hotel, since all I wanted was to go back to my room. I barely ate my food, then asked to leave before dessert or coffee.

We didn't speak the whole way back to the Mistletoe Inn. Zeke looked like he was feeling as awful as I did. When we got back to the hotel he pulled up to the front door and I immediately reached for the door handle.

"Kim," he said. "I didn't mean to hurt your feelings. I was only trying to help."

I opened the door, climbed out of the car, then turned back to him. "Thank you for your help." I turned and walked away. When I got to my room I threw my manuscript against the wall, scattering it in a mess of pages. Then I fell on the bed and cried.

Chapter

Twenty-one

*Too many times we lose today's
battles because we're still engaged
in fighting yesterday's.*

Kimberly Rossi's Diary

I didn't sleep well, and I didn't exercise the next morning. I didn't want to take the chance I'd see Zeke. I was embarrassed about how I had handled things. The worst part was that I wasn't even sure why it hurt so much. I knew that he hadn't wanted to hurt me. For that matter, why did I even care? Who's to say that he knew any more than anyone else? What I did know was that being with him had been the best part of the conference so far. Why had I ruined it?

I ordered breakfast from room service, then, after eating, climbed into the tub, where I stayed until the water started to turn cold. I got out and went back to bed, purposely missing the workshop. Today we were supposed to share our partners' critiques of our books, and the thought of that was about as welcome as a kidney stone.

Also, today was my day to meet with the agents, and I didn't want to face them already bloodied. Besides, maybe they'd disagree with Zeke and the whole thing would be moot.

I finally got out of bed around eleven. I dressed and did my hair, then went down to find Samantha. As I walked out into the lobby Zeke was sitting on one of the sofas. He immediately stood. "Kim."

I started to turn away from him.

"Kim, please, talk to me."

In spite of my regret, seeing him brought back the pain. Again my feelings overcame me. "Why? You found more things wrong with my book?"

He put his hand on my arm. "Look, I know how much it hurts to be criticized. Trust me, I've had more than my share. But all criticism isn't the same. Some criticism is mean-spirited and some is shared because someone cares. It's like . . . telling a friend they have something in their teeth."

"In this scenario I'm your slob friend with something in her teeth?"

He raised his hands as if in surrender. "I'm sorry, bad example. I know last night shook you up, but it should have encouraged you."

My eyes welled up. "Encouraged me to do what? Quit? Trust me, don't get a job as an inspirational speaker, because you suck at it."

His brow furrowed. "You're not going to let me apologize, are you?"

Even though I could see how much he was hurting, I said nothing. Finally he breathed out slowly. "All right, I'll leave you alone. Good luck. I hope things go well for you when you meet with the agents today. I hope they're kinder than I am." He turned and walked away.

As I watched him go a tear fell down my

cheek. I felt sick inside. The moment I let myself be vulnerable, I got hurt. When would I learn?

As I sat there, Samantha walked up to me. "You'll never believe what the brilliant work- shop group F talked about today. Love and *wormholes,* and would it be ethically wrong to be in love with two different people if they lived in different dimensions. Honestly, I wanted to puncture my eardrums." She stopped. "Are you okay? You look like you've been crying."

I looked down so she couldn't see my eyes.

"Honey, what's wrong?"

After a moment I shook my head. "Nothing. Let's just go to lunch."

At the table Samantha just stared at me. "Talk to me. What's going on?"

I took a deep breath. "You know I let Zeke read my book."

"And?"

"He didn't like it."

She blinked slowly. "And he told you that? I knew I didn't like him. For the record, he doesn't really look like George Clooney, I was just being nice. He looks more like George Costanza on *Seinfeld.*"

"No he doesn't," I said, suddenly feeling protective of him. "He's beautiful. And he's sweet. He was just being honest."

Samantha frowned. "How can he tell you your book stinks and still be sweet?"

"He didn't say it stinks. He had constructive criticism."

"Now you're defending him? This is like that Stockholm syndrome."

"This is nothing like Stockholm syndrome."

"It's some kind of syndrome," she said. "So what do you do now?"

"I don't know. He tried to apologize, twice, but I . . ." I took a deep breath. "I'll probably never see him again."

"I'm sorry," she said. "But cheer up. Don't you have your agents this afternoon?"

"Yes."

"Good. Let me tell you what's going to happen. You're going to knock their socks off. And Zeke is going to be eating his words with catsup and French-fried potatoes."

I just looked at her. She was the strangest and sweetest person I'd ever met.

"I love you," I said.

She smiled. "I love you too," she said, then added, "in a totally non-romantic way."

"Thanks for the disclaimer."

She kissed me on the cheek. "Anytime, sweetie. Anytime."

Chapter
Twenty-two

*There's no point in switching course
after you've hit the iceberg.*

Kimberly Rossi's Diary

The way the agent meetings worked was fairly standard for these kinds of conferences. I paid—actually my father had paid—a hundred dollars to meet with each agent. I gave the agent a copy of my manuscript, which he or she was obligated to read for fifteen minutes and then write a brief assessment.

The first agent I met with was Timothy Ryan, a twenty-seven-year veteran of the publishing industry. We met in a room with five other agents and authors.

As I settled nervously into my chair, Timothy looked down at his appointment list, then back at me. "You're Kimberly Rossi."

"Yes, sir."

"Just a moment." He fanned through a pile of papers, then stopped on one. He looked over the paper, presumably his notes on my book, then back up at me with a stern, tense expression. "Your book is *The Mistletoe Promise*?"

"Yes, sir."

"Is this the first book you've written?"

"Yes, sir. Can you tell?"

He just nodded slowly as he looked back down at his summary. He hesitated a moment, then said, "Obviously with our time constraints, I'm

216

prohibited from giving you a complete evaluation of your work, but let me say this—I love the concept of your book, but there are two things that would keep it from selling to a publisher.

"First, your character development needs improve-ment. Specifically, your characters are too perfect. No one's going to relate to someone that Pollyannaish. They need some skeletons in their closets, if you know what I mean." He gazed at me, waiting for a response.

"I think so."

"Second, I'm just not feeling *it*."

I just looked at him for a moment, then said, "You're not feeling . . . what?"

"The passion," he said, gesturing with his hand. "The 'it.' I think you're holding back, and you need to dig deeper. No one wants to read about a perfect life. There's no interest in the mundane. The masses of readers buy romances because they want to see flawed people healed by love, you know what I mean?" Again he skewered me with his gaze.

"Someone told me that last night."

"Well, you should listen to her. My feeling is, you can write, but I think you can do better than this. This novel almost feels like you're faking the emotion. You need to take it up a few notches." He took a business card out of his pocket and handed it to me. "I'm going to do something I rarely do. Here's my contact information. Do not share this with anyone at this conference. You can send me your manuscript after you've fixed it, and I'll give it another read. Like I said, I think you've got a great concept, and I think you have talent. If you're able to make the changes I recommended, I might be able to do something with it." He glanced down at his watch. "We're out of time."

I put the card in my purse, then slowly stood. "Thank you," I said.

"Don't mention it. Good luck."

My next agent meeting was less encouraging but not dissimilar in tone. The agent was a woman named Rachel Bestor. She was a former editor for Hay House turned romance agent.

"It's not doing anything for me," she said bluntly. "Your protagonist, this Elise woman, she's like a Girl Scout. Throw some dirt on her. Or show us her dirt. You're not a bad writer, but this book doesn't prove it."

I walked away from the meetings more upset that I had wasted my father's money than bothered by what the agents had to say. They had, essentially, told me the exact same things that Zeke had, yet I hadn't blown up at them. And Zeke was much nicer about it.

I guess, in my heart, I knew that what Zeke was saying was true. Suddenly I understood why I had been so hurt by him. Deep inside I wasn't listening for his critique of my book, I was listening for his critique of me. I never should have confused the two.

After meeting with the agents I felt obligated to call my father, which, as much as I dreaded it, I did the moment I got back to my room.

"How's the conference?" he asked.

"Good," I said. "I met with the agents today."

"How did it go?"

"It wasn't what I hoped. They weren't interested in representing my book. I'm sorry I wasted your money."

"Did they give you any hope of being published?"

"They both said I was a good writer. I mean, maybe they say that to everyone, but they seemed sincere."

"How are you handling it?"

"You know how badly I handle rejection. How are you doing?"

"Hanging in there," he said. "I've been feeling pretty tired. I had to cancel the motorcycle ride."

"I'm sorry," I said.

"It's just for now. I'll get that surgery and be back in the saddle. And that's what I expect of you. Get back in the saddle. I didn't raise a quitter."

I suddenly felt like a little girl again. "All right, Dad."

"Other than this speed bump, have you had a good time? Have you learned anything?"

"It's been a good conference. It's been fun."

"Have you made any new friends?"

"A few."

"That's good. You could use some new friends." After a moment of silence he said, "You know I believe in you."

"I know. Thanks, Dad. I'll talk to you soon. I love you."

"I love you more," he said. Before hanging up he threw out once more, "Get back in the saddle."

The moment I hung up I dialed the hotel operator.

"Hello, Ms. Rossi. How may I help you?"

"Could you connect me with one of your guests, please?"

"Of course, which room?"

"I don't know his room number. It's Zeke Faulkner."

"Faulkner," she repeated. "Just a moment, please."

The phone rang at least half a dozen times before Zeke answered. "Hello." He sounded a little groggy, as if he'd been napping.

"Zeke, it's Kim."

"Hi," he said cautiously.

"Did I wake you?"

"Yes."

"I met with the agents today."

He was quiet for a moment, then obligingly asked, "How did it go?"

"They said what you did."

He said nothing, which was even worse than an "I told you so."

I took a deep breath and pressed on. "I called to say I'm sorry about how I acted last night. And today. I know I don't deserve it, but if you're willing . . . may we go to dinner tonight? I'll pay . . . Or maybe we could just talk."

He still said nothing.

I sat there for a moment in silence, then said, "All right. I know you want to punish me, and I deserve it. But please don't. Please?"

I heard him breathe out.

"Okay, I'll say it. I'm an idiot and I'm not as smart as you. And I'm overly emotional. Is that what you want to hear?"

He exhaled. "No. That's not what I wanted to hear. I would never say those things. Good night, Kim."

"Good night," I said weakly.

I slowly hung up the phone, hating myself. A dark little voice inside of me said, *You sabotage everything. No wonder nobody wants you. You deserve to be alone for the rest of your life.*

Chapter
Twenty-three

The problem with the past is that too often yesterday's lessons were meant for yesterday's problems.

Kimberly Rossi's Diary

I tried to read but instead I mostly just lay on the bed and cried for the next half hour until my phone rang. I crawled over and answered it.

"Hello."

"All right," Zeke said softly. "Let's talk."

I wiped back my tears. "Okay. Where?"

"I'll meet you in the lobby in five minutes. Bring your coat."

I stood waiting in the lobby for what seemed a long time, wondering if he'd changed his mind. Then he came out of the elevator. He walked up to me, looking solemn but not angry. "Come," he said. He took my hand and led me toward the front doors. "Let's go for a walk."

We walked away from the inn down the long, rutted drive, lit by the sparkling yellow-white lights of wrapped evergreens. The stars were bright above us and the night air was freezing and moist. We had walked maybe fifty yards when I said, "I'm really sorry."

"Why are you sorry?" he asked.

I didn't know if he was really asking or if he was making me own up to my bad behavior. "I was mean to you. You were only trying to help."

He nodded. "I was trying to help."

"The agents said the exact same thing you did.

Only you were kinder." I looked at him. "How did you know what they'd say?"

"It's always easier to critique from the outside," he said. "You would have seen it if it wasn't your own book." His voice seemed lighter. Forgiving.

"I feel so embarrassed."

"No one wants to hear criticism. I don't."

I swallowed. "I don't think I was really angry about the book."

"I know."

I looked at him quizzically. "How did you know?"

"Because every book is about its author. You felt attacked by me, even though I wasn't attacking you. You were fighting shadows."

I looked into his eyes. "What does my book say about me?"

"You're writing about a fake romance, one in which the characters draw up a contract to define the relationship." He looked into my eyes. "You've been hurt and you want a guarantee that you won't be hurt again."

I just nodded.

"It's understandable," he continued. "You're afraid to put your hand back on the stove. That's not weakness, that's intelligence. But wisdom is knowing that we need love and knowing when it's safe and whom to trust."

"It seems like it's never safe," I said.

"I know," he said softly. "But it's an illusion. The thing is, we use past relationships like maps to navigate new ones. But it doesn't work that way, because every human, every relationship is different. It's like trying to use a map of Las Vegas to get around Vermont. It won't work. That's why so many people get lost." He looked at me. "I don't know everything that's happened to you in your life, but I think there's more to your hurts than your divorce and failed engagements. I think there's something deeper you're afraid of."

I stopped walking and looked at him. "What's that?"

He looked deeply into my eyes, then said, "I think you doubt that you're worthy of love."

For a while I couldn't speak. I was afraid to look at him. When I finally did he was looking at me lovingly. "Let me tell you something I want you to never forget." He leaned forward until our faces were inches apart, then I closed my eyes as he pulled me into him and kissed me. When we finally parted I was breathless. He said to me, "No matter what anyone says or does, you are worthy of love. You always have been. You always will be. And I'm safe for you. You can trust me."

Then he pulled me back into him. As we kissed, tears rolled down my cheeks. I had never felt so loved.

Chapter
Twenty-four

My life has been filled with surprises.
Far too few of them were welcome.

Kimberly Rossi's Diary

The next morning Zeke knocked on my door around nine. I opened it wearing an oversized T-shirt and my sexiest pink sweatpants.

"Good morning," I said, the smile from the night before still lingering.

He leaned forward and we kissed. "What are you doing today?" he asked.

"More of this, I hope."

He smiled. "I meant the conference. Is there anything you can't miss?"

"That depends on the offer."

"I thought we'd spend the day together. I want to take you somewhere."

"Somewhere?"

He nodded. "Somewhere."

"I have to get dressed."

"Okay. But hurry."

"Why do I need to hurry?"

"Because we have a very tight schedule to keep."

"Can I have a half hour?"

"I can give you twenty minutes," he said. "I'll be in the lobby. And dress warm."

"I'll hurry," I said.

Fifteen minutes later I walked out into the lobby. Zeke was standing next to the front doors checking his phone messages. He looked up at me and smiled. "That was fast."

"Where are you taking me?" I asked, offering him my hand.

"Someplace Christmasy," he said.

"I don't like Christmas."

"I know."

"Is *Christmasy* even a word?"

"If you understood it, it's a word."

"Really, where are we going?"

"Remember what I said last night about trust?"

"Yes."

"This is where you show that you trust me."

"Okay," I said. "I'm all yours."

Outside, a pristine, crystalline blanket of snow lay snugly across the grounds of the resort, shimmering beneath the morning sun. Zeke's car was waiting for us just a few yards from the front doors. He retrieved the key from the valet, opened my door for me, then we sped away.

A half hour into our drive I asked, "Are we going back to Burlington?"

"Sort of."

"What does that mean?"

"It means we're going to Burlington so we can leave Burlington."

"Now I'm more confused."

"We're flying out."

"Really?"

"You'll enjoy this," he said.

"I should have called Samantha," I said. "She thinks we're having lunch."

He smiled.

We parked the car in the airport's covered parking lot, then hurried through the terminal. As we approached the check-in counter, I said, "May I ask where we're going besides someplace 'Christmasy'?"

"Bethlehem."

"Israel?"

"Bethlehem, Pennsylvania. Christmas City, USA."

A half hour later we boarded the first-class section of the plane. We flew from Burlington into Newark, then took a smaller plane into ABE, the Lehigh Valley International Airport in Allentown, Pennsylvania. In all, our flights were less than three hours and we arrived at our destination around four in the afternoon.

"Let me tell you about Bethlehem," Zeke said. "It was named Bethlehem on Christmas Eve 1741 before America was even a country. They have one of the most famous Christmas markets in America called the Christkindlmarkt. There's music and shops, artisans, and really great food. I think you're going to love it."

We took a cab from Allentown and it was already starting to get dark as we pulled into the

Christmas village in the center of the Bethlehem Historic District. The streets were beautifully lit for the season and crowded with tourists. In the center of the town we passed a massive Christmas tree.

As I got out of the taxi, my senses were assaulted by the sweet-smelling wares of the outdoor vendors—candied nuts, kettle corn, caramel-dipped fruits and chocolate—all sharing the crisp air with the sounds of school and church choirs and street musicians.

We stopped on one corner to listen to an elderly man dressed in army fatigues and a thick army jacket play "Winter Wonderland" on a saxophone. Zeke tipped him a twenty-dollar bill and the man was so pleased that he asked Zeke if he could play a request for his "lovely lady." I asked him to play "Silver Bells," which he did beautifully. Zeke gave him another twenty.

For dinner we stopped at a little German shop and had a meal of bratwurst with sauerkraut and cheese-beer soup, and to drink we had Glühwein, a delicious hot red wine seasoned with mulling spices and raisins.

I don't know if it was more the wine or my heart, but I was intoxicated. The mood around the city matched the music inside of me and I felt jovial and festive and free. I hadn't had that much fun for as long as I could remember. Especially not at Christmas.

For several hours we wandered among the booths of artisans, admiring their creations. We spent time watching a glassblower and Zeke bought me a glass ornament to commemorate the evening.

As the night waned it occurred to me that we wouldn't be going back to Vermont. "Where are we staying tonight?"

"The Waldorf Astoria."

"There's a Waldorf Astoria in Bethlehem?"

"No. It's in New York."

"We're spending the night in New York?"

"Have you ever been there?"

"No. I've always wanted to. When are we going back to the conference?"

"Tomorrow night," he said. He smiled. "Don't worry, you'll be back in time to hear your beloved author and get your book signed."

"You didn't tell me we were spending the night. I don't have anything to change into."

"I think you might be able to find something to wear in New York," he said. "I'll take you to Saks Fifth Avenue as soon as they open."

I looked at him. "Why are we going to New York?"

"It's Christmasy," he replied.

"Christmasy," I repeated.

"You wrote about New York in your book. I thought you ought to at least go there and take some notes. It's always better to see what you're writing about. Otherwise you miss the details that really make a book. Like where we are now. Smell the air. What do you smell?"

I took in a deep breath. "Cinnamon and sugar, from the man over there making candied almonds. And I smell wassail."

He smiled. "Details, details. Books are like life. It's all in the details."

Zeke had booked a sedan, a white-pearl Lincoln Town Car, to drive us to New York. I hated to leave Bethlehem, but I was excited to finally see Manhattan. The ride was about two hours but it didn't seem that long. I wished it would have been longer. Much longer. The steel-gray leather-upholstered seat of the car was soft and spacious, and Zeke held me the entire way.

About forty minutes out of Manhattan we began to kiss and we didn't stop until the car stopped on Park Avenue at the front doors of the Waldorf a little after midnight. The driver had to clear his throat to announce that we'd reached our destina-tion. Zeke had the most delicious kisses.

I had wondered if Zeke had planned for us to share the same room, but I should have known better. He was a gentleman. Still, I have to admit that I was a little disappointed. We kissed some more, then said good night. After I closed the door to my room I thought of calling my father to tell him where I was, but I quickly decided against it. Based on my history with men, he'd want to know all about Zeke and he would probably hate him before he even knew him. I didn't want my father to hate him.

As I lay in my luxurious bed surrounded by the opulence of the hotel and the sounds of a city that never slept, I took in a deep breath and smiled. My face was slightly warm and stubble burned from all our kissing and I liked the feel of it. This may have been the best day of my life. And there was still tomorrow. It wasn't often that I looked forward to tomorrow.

Chapter
Twenty-five

To be in love is something.
To be loved is everything.

Kimberly Rossi's Diary

New York during the holidays is like a Christmas show with a million extras. Zeke woke me early and, wearing our hotel robes, we ate breakfast together in my room. Then I showered and put my only clothes back on and we walked to Saks Fifth Avenue. Zeke bought me more than just an outfit for the day. He spent more than a thousand dollars.

Then he took me to Tiffany and bought me a beautiful rose-gold "Return to Tiffany" heart tag pendant with a gold chain. He wanted to spend more on a different necklace, but I had always wanted a simple Tiffany heart, so against my protests, he bought me a matching heart bracelet to go with it instead.

As we were riding the elevator down from the second floor, Zeke asked, "Have you ever seen a Broadway show?"

"I've seen *Jersey Boys*," I said. "In Vegas."

"I liked *Jersey Boys*," he said. "Who doesn't like Frankie Valli? Is there anything else you've wanted to see?"

"Hypothetically speaking?"

"Yes."

"I've always wanted to see *Wicked*. Have you seen it?"

"A few times. I got to see it with the original

cast." He took his phone out of his pocket. "Just look around for a minute. I need to make a call."

I browsed through the first floor's glass jewelry cases for about ten minutes before Zeke returned. "I've got us matinee tickets to *Wicked*," he announced.

"How did you do that? Aren't they sold out months in advance?"

"I know people," he said.

Two hours later we were sitting in the second row in the middle section of the Gershwin Theatre.

The show was as good as I hoped it would be. Afterward, Zeke bought me a "Defy Gravity" T-shirt and took me to dinner at a wonderful historic restaurant called Keens Steakhouse.

"You should put this place in your book," Zeke said. "It's got great history. Do you know who's dined here?" Before I could guess he said, "Teddy Roosevelt, Babe Ruth, Will Rogers, Albert Einstein, General Douglas MacArthur, 'Buffalo Bill' Cody, pretty much the who's who of humanity." He smiled. "And Kimberly Rossi. Someday they'll boast about you. One of America's great writers."

I couldn't help but smile.

For dinner I ordered a petite filet mignon and a crab cocktail and Zeke ordered prime rib. As we ate Zeke asked, "Did you enjoy the show?"

"I loved the show."

"I know Gregory Maguire."

"Who?"

"Gregory Maguire. He's the author of *Wicked*. Did you know how he came up with the name of Elphaba?"

"No."

"It comes from L. F. B., the initials of L. Frank Baum, the author of *The Wizard of Oz*. And, for the record, Gregory has a beautiful singing voice."

"Okay, you're blowing my mind," I said. "First it's Catherine McCullin and R. L. Stine, now Gregory Maguire. How do you know these people?"

"Writers' conferences," he said. "I used to go to them all the time."

"I went to a writers' conference with Mary Higgins Clark, but we're not best friends."

"I never said we're best friends. I'm just good at making acquaintances."

"Like me?" I asked.

His expression immediately turned. "No. Not like you. Do you think I'm just playing around with you?"

"Honestly, I don't know what you're doing with me," I said softly.

He was quiet for a moment, then his expression relaxed. "I'm sorry. Of course you don't. You don't even know me." He took a deep breath. "I don't often get close to people, especially women. But this time I have." He looked into my eyes. "I'm afraid I've fallen in love."

Chapter
Twenty-six

The reason we cage the past is sometimes only understood after we un-cage it.

Kimberly Rossi's Diary

It was a short flight back to Vermont. We flew out of LaGuardia at nine and our plane landed in Burlington just a little after ten-thirty. We retrieved Zeke's car and headed back to the inn. It wasn't quite midnight when we arrived and Zeke parked his rental car just short of the portico, leaving it running to keep the heater on.

After leaning over and kissing him I said, "I'm curious, how hard was it to plan all that?"

"It was simple."

"That was *simple?*" I said doubtfully. "We flew to Bethlehem, drove to New York, spent the night in the Waldorf Astoria, shopped Fifth Avenue, took in a Broadway show, had a fabulous dinner, then flew back to Vermont, and you call that simple?"

"Very simple," he said. "I'm a simple guy."

"*You* really think you're simple?"

"I *know* I'm simple," he said. "What you see is what you get."

"You're a lot of things, but you're definitely not simple. You're an enigma wrapped in a mystery, or whatever Churchill said."

"Really. What's enigmatic about me?"

"The mind reels," I said.

"Go on," he said. "What makes me enigmatic?"

"Okay, to begin with, why are you single? Why would any woman in her right mind leave you? It would be like driving a Rolls-Royce over a cliff. You're the whole package. You're kind, you're fun, you're smart, and you kiss like a Hoover vacuum cleaner . . ."

One brow rose. "Is that a good thing?"

"That's a good thing," I said. "You're very, very good-looking . . ."

"Thank you."

"I'm not done," I said. "You must have a lot of money, but you're not obsessed with it. And you know more about books than anyone I've met, but you aren't published. So no, you're not as simple as you think you are. In fact, you're so complex it's scary."

"Scary?" he said. "In one minute I went from 'not simple' to 'enigmatic' to 'scary.' Explain scary."

"They say if it's too good to be true, it is. You should have that yellow caution tape wrapped all around you, because you're way too good to be true."

"I'll take that as a compliment."

"I don't know if it is one," I said. "Because *too good to be true* leaves a lot of questions unanswered."

"Such as?"

"The big one?"

He just gazed at me with an amused smile. "If

241

you have a question, just ask. I'll give you a simple answer."

"Okay, here's the big one." I took a deep breath as he looked at me in anticipation.

"Go on," he said.

"I'm building up to it. It's a big question."

He grinned.

"Here goes. Why do you like me?"

He looked at me. "That's it? That's all you got?"

"Yes."

"Simple. Pretty much for every reason you just said about me. You're kind, smart, funny, fun, grateful, and beautiful.

"And to answer your question, why am I single? Because until now, I've chosen to be. There have been other women in my life and many of them have been smart and stunningly beautiful and yes, at my age, chemistry is still important. But something about my chemistry has changed. I've found that when someone is beautiful on the outside but spiritually dark inside, all that outer beauty is just lipstick on a pig."

I smiled at the metaphor.

His tone turned more serious. "When I was younger and more full of myself, I wanted to be with the cool people—the clever, arrogant ones with the snarky comebacks and designer clothes. And then life went on and I saw how they treated others. And me. Eventually, I got sick of their pretense and their fraudulent personalities. Frankly, I didn't want to be with someone who was that much work.

"And I didn't want to entrust my heart to women who were so full of themselves that they could hardly see me through their Gucci sunglasses. I wanted someone real. Someone who would laugh at the same stupid things I laugh at and think it's fun to stop in a little café and eat bratwurst and beer-cheese soup. I wanted someone who would worry if she had hurt someone's feelings or would help a complete stranger."

I thought about what he was saying. "You mean like the hearing-impaired woman in our workshop."

"Exactly," he said. "That's when I knew you were more than a pretty face. You were the only one who noticed that she was struggling. But you didn't just notice, you spoke up and changed seats with her. You showed compassion." He looked down for a moment, then back up. "That's what my wife would have done."

I looked at him softly. "You speak almost reverently of your wife," I said. "But she left you. Why did she leave?"

He was quiet for a moment, then said, "It wasn't her choice to leave. She was five months pregnant when she had a hemorrhage in the night and died. I wasn't with her. I should have been, but I wasn't. I was away on a business trip. I wasn't there when she needed me." His eyes welled up. "Now you know my simple truth."

As I looked at him my eyes filled with tears too. I pulled him in to me and, for a moment, just held him against my breast. Then I said, "There's something I need to tell you too."

Sensing the gravity of my tone he sat back up.

"When you said the other night that you felt I was hiding something, you were right." I took a deep breath and leaned back to look into his eyes. "My mother didn't die of cancer. She committed suicide."

Zeke frowned. "I'm sorry."

"You're the first person I've ever told that to. Ever. I didn't even tell my husband."

"He didn't know how your mother died?"

"No. But he wouldn't have cared anyway."

He continued to look at me sympathetically.

"As long as I knew her she struggled with depression. By the time she killed herself, it was her fifth attempt. The first time she tried I blamed myself. I wasn't even ten years old and I was certain that it was my fault.

"By her third attempt, I was eleven, and my feelings had changed. I was scared and confused, but more than that, I was angry. I wondered how I could mean so little to her that she could just leave me. What does that say about me?" I looked at him. "I've carried the shame of her abandonment my entire life.

"Since then I've looked for validation of myself in every relationship and ended up holding so tight that I squeezed the life out of them. I just wanted someone to prove to me that I was worth sticking around for. I wanted to know that I was worth loving. But the more I chased it, the faster it fled. Knowing your self-worth isn't something others can validate. You either believe it or you don't. I never have."

"Faith," he said softly. "Having a sense of self-worth is an act of faith." He looked at me for a moment, then said, "Kim, your mother wasn't running from you. She was running from herself. When someone's depressed, it's like they're trapped in a burning high-rise. No one wants to jump out of a sixteenth-floor window, but if it's that or be burned alive, they don't feel like they have a choice. I know."

"How do you know?"

"I'm not as far removed from it as you might think."

Something about what he'd said filled me with fear. "What do you mean?"

"I read somewhere that authors are twice as likely to commit suicide than the average person." He looked into my eyes. "They're right."

Fear's grip tightened. "What are you saying?"

He hesitated for a moment, then said, "It

was right after my wife died when I tried to kill myself."

"What?"

"I tried to kill myself by overdosing on painkillers. I was revived at the hospital. I'm alive today because I botched my suicide attempt."

At that moment something happened to me. Something I couldn't explain and couldn't resist. An evil slithered from the darkest recesses of my mind, a fear I hadn't felt since childhood, a thick black serpent that wrapped around my chest, cinching tighter and tighter until I couldn't breathe. I couldn't speak. I couldn't think.

At that moment I wasn't in Vermont. I was a little girl standing in the doorway of her mother's bedroom looking at the blood running down her mother's arms, screaming at her to put down the knife. Everything around me turned to white. I began shaking uncontrollably. "No."

Zeke reached out for me. "Kim . . . what's going on?"

"No," I said, suddenly drawing away from him. "No. I can't do this. I can't go through that again."

"Kim, I'm not suicidal. Listen to me. It was a really hard time."

"Life is always hard. It's always hard. I can't do it. I can't." Tears ran down my cheeks in a steady current. I felt like the world was spinning. I felt nauseous. "I'm so sorry, I can't."

"Things are different now. It was a phase. A dark phase."

My body was shaking and I began rocking back and forth. "I'm so sorry. I'm so sorry. I'm so sorry. I'm so sorry."

"Kim, I won't leave you. Ever. I promise."

I covered my eyes with my hand. "I'm sorry. I can't believe you. There are no promises in hell." Leaving my bags of presents, I opened the car door and ran into the hotel.

The night was a blank. I don't remember going back to my room. I don't remember getting undressed or hiding under the covers. All I remember was darkness.

Chapter
Twenty-seven

Why must I prove to myself over and over that I am my own worst enemy?

Kimberly Rossi's Diary

The conference was over. Everything was over. I woke to someone knocking on my door. "Kim? Honey?"

I lay in bed with the lights out, the closed shutters glowing from the morning sun. I felt as if I had an emotional hangover. I didn't want to see anyone. I wanted the outside world to just go away. I wanted to go away.

"Kim, it's Samantha. Are you there? I'm going to call security."

"Hold on," I said, groaning. I got up, pulled on a robe, then walked to the door, opening it just enough to peer out.

Samantha looked at me with a concerned expression. I'm sure I looked awful. "Honey, where have you been?"

"I went away with Zeke."

"Did he do something to you?"

"No. I left him."

"May I come in?"

I moved back from the door. Samantha stepped into the room and put her arms around me. "I'm so sorry."

After a minute I asked, "Do you know what day it is?"

"It's Monday," she said.

"What time is it?"

"It's almost nine. Hotel check-out time is eleven. And I have news. Cowell's confirmed. He's speaking at noon. What time is your flight home?"

My mind was so jumbled that it took me a moment to remember. "Three, three ten. Something like that." I sat down on the corner of the bed. Samantha sat next to me. She took my hand and held it in her lap.

"I don't even care if I see him," I said.

"Zeke?"

"Cowell," I said.

"Of course you do," Samantha said. "You've waited years for this. You're not going to miss it. I won't let you."

"I just can't go out."

"No," she said. "You're going through with this. No excuses, no regrets. You'll be angry at yourself if you miss it."

After a minute I took a deep breath. "All right."

"All right you'll go with me to his speech?"

I nodded. "I still need to get ready and pack."

"Okay. I'll go save us some seats."

"It's not until noon."

"There's already a line. This is going to be huge. So don't you dare stand me up. I'll be inside the ballroom waiting for you with a seat."

"I'll be there."

"Promise?"

"I promise."

She hugged me. "I'm sorry things didn't work out." She kissed me on the cheek, then walked out of the room.

I lay back for almost twenty minutes, then undressed and went in to shower. I sat under the hot water for a long time, trying to avoid a panic attack. My mind was a labyrinth of thoughts. I had waited years to meet H. T. Cowell. So why was my mind fixated on another man?

Chapter
Twenty-eight

Ironically, what makes an author popular is not shouting to the masses but rather quiet, solitary whispers.

Kimberly Rossi's Diary

More than two hours before Cowell's speech the room was already filled to capacity. There were at least quadruple the number of people in the room than had even attended the conference. I knew that Cowell's return was a big deal to me, but I had failed to realize that it was a big deal to millions of people—like *finding Jimmy Hoffa's body* big. There were television cameras lining both walls of the ballroom and at least a couple dozen photographers sitting on the floor in front of the dais.

I looked around for Samantha for nearly ten minutes, finally finding her in the front row. "How did you get front-row seats?" I asked.

"When I left your room they had the ballroom doors locked and there was already a long line to get in, so I sneaked in through the employee service entrance."

"You were serious about getting a good seat," I said.

"I did it for you," she said. "After the man bomb I thought you needed it."

"Thank you."

"My pleasure," she said. "How are you feeling now?"

I couldn't answer. My eyes immediately started to well up.

"Still bad," she said. "I'm sorry. Love's a mess."

"Then why are we romance writers?"

"Someone needs to clean it up."

People continued to crowd into the ballroom, and still there were long lines outside the ballroom doors. Then a fire marshal walked into the room, and security began turning people away.

The excitement in the room was palpable. At noon the lights went down and the room fell into a hush. A single spotlight cast a broad light on the podium. Then there was a slight ripple of light on the curtain and I could see that someone was walking behind it, looking for the opening. Then a single hand reached out.

I once spoke to someone who had been to a Beatles concert at the height of Beatlemania. She said as the curtain lifted just enough to reveal the Beatles' feet and ankles, girls began fainting around her. That's what it felt like. Even with my heart aching, I could feel the collective energy in the room just waiting to explode. Suddenly the curtain parted.

"There he is," Samantha said.

The entire room fell into total silence as the curtain was pulled back and a man emerged from the darkness. For a moment I was speechless. It was him.

Chapter

Twenty-nine

The difference between fiction and nonfiction is that fiction must follow rules of legitimacy. Reality doesn't.

Kimberly Rossi's Diary

H. T. Cowell looked the way I envisioned Tolstoy would look. He wasn't tall but he was dignified and straight and, as Zeke had ventured, old. He wore round wire-rimmed glasses and his hair and the beard that covered his entire chin were almost white. He walked slowly to the podium. For just a moment the audience was silent as the sound of his footsteps echoed in the room. Then the assault of the paparazzi began. The electric clicking and whirring of cameras was accompanied by bright, staccato flashes.

"You were right," Samantha said. "He's old."

"He's ancient," I said. "But he looks . . . right."

He was immaculately dressed in clothes that appeared custom tailored: dark wool slacks, a cashmere jacket, and an oxford shirt, which he wore open without a tie. As he stepped up to the microphone it seemed that the world around me disappeared. But it wasn't just me who had fallen into a trance; everyone seemed similarly hypnotized. The experience was like waiting for a monk who had taken a lifetime vow of silence to speak his first word. We waited in breathless anticipation.

He took a square piece of paper from his breast pocket, unfolded it, and set it on the lectern. Then he lightly tapped the microphone, cleared his throat, and leaned forward until his lips were nearly on the appliance.

"Is this working?" he asked gruffly into the microphone. There were a few audible responses from the back of the room and he nodded. "Thank you."

He stood rigid as a signpost as he slowly surveyed the room with an unmistakable confidence, as if he were still deciding whether or not the congregation was worthy of him. Then he leaned forward again.

"Books are important things."

The simple words reverberated with authority throughout the darkened room. It was like God had spoken.

"Books are more than paper and glue and ink. They are more than digital imprints. They are sparks. Sparks that ignite fires. Sparks that ignite revolutions. Every major revolution began with a book." He looked around the room again as if ensuring that every eye was on him. They were.

"Every major religious revolution started with a book. The Bible, the Talmud, the Koran, the Tipitaka, the Tao Te Ching, the Book of Mormon, *Dianetics*—all these faiths have books at their foundations. Billions of people have followed a specific life path because of a book.

"Every political revolution began with a book. From John Stuart Mill's *On Liberty* to Karl

Marx's *Communist Manifesto* to Hitler's *Mein Kampf.*

"Every cultural and societal revolution began with a book. Harriet Beecher Stowe's *Uncle Tom's Cabin*, the book that Abraham Lincoln said started a very big war, not only ignited the Civil War but led to the ongoing war for civil rights, not just for blacks in America, but for all races. Then there's Rachel Carson's *Silent Spring*, which began the green movement.

"These powerful, world-changing books did not spontaneously appear. They were not conceived by committee or board. They were created in one mind, by one author. Many of you are here today because you desire to be an author. You may not have understood the power or implications of your desire, but you have desired well.

"But greater than the desire to be an author is the desire to write something of consequence. To write truth. Such an author is rare." He again cleared his throat. "Perhaps it is a good thing, though. The world can only handle so much revolution." He stopped and took several gulps from a bottle of water. "When such writers come along, we should revere them. We should understand that we are in the presence of greatness.

"That is why I'm especially honored today to introduce an author who has written truths that have captured the world's imagination. I am honored to introduce Mr. H. T. Cowell."

A discernible gasp rose from the audience. Someone behind me said out loud what I was thinking, likely what we were all thinking. *That's not Cowell?*

Samantha leaned into me. "It's not him. That's not Cowell."

The man continued. "H. T. Cowell is one of those rare breeds of authors who has made a difference in this world. His first book, *The Tuscan Promise*, defined a genre and launched a thousand writers and ten thousand imitations.

"A lesser mind might attempt to discount the influence of Cowell's works by saying he only wrote romance. *Only*. As if romance were of no consequence. Romance is the thing that dreams are made of and all great human endeavors are borne of dreams."

He paused, and again his gaze panned the audience. "Ladies and gentlemen, it is my profound honor to give you H. T. Cowell."

The entire audience rose to their feet, including me. For a moment there was no one. Then the curtain parted. Zeke walked out onto the stage.

Chapter

Thirty

Sometimes we think we know the author from his book, only to learn that we didn't even know his book.

Kimberly Rossi's Diary

Zeke hugged the speaker, who turned and walked back to the curtain. Zeke followed the man with his gaze, then turned back to the audience, which was still applauding wildly. Except for me. I couldn't move.

"Thank you," he said, raising his hand. "Thank you. You're too kind. Please sit down." The applause only slightly diminished. "Please."

It took several minutes before everyone sat.

"I'd like to thank my agent, Mr. Harvey Yospe, for that eloquent, not-so-modest introduction." His eyes scanned the audience as if he were looking for someone. Then his eyes met mine. I was frozen. He held my gaze for a moment, then turned away.

"It's been a while since I've stood before an audience. A long while. I've missed this.

"I don't title my speeches like I do my books, but I noticed that the hosts of this noble event have saved me the trouble. They appropriately named my talk *Why I Stopped Writing*. So that is what I will talk about.

"I will never forget the day that Mr. Yospe called me at my home in Bethlehem, Pennsylvania. Rarely in life does our reality exceed our dreams. For me, that was the first of many such days. At the time I was a high school English teacher with a very modest salary. To celebrate our good fortune my wife, Emma, and I splurged. I took her to Pizza Hut."

The audience laughed.

"The book he was interested in was *The Tuscan Promise*. Three weeks after I hired Mr. Yospe as my agent, the roller coaster began. My book went into a publisher's auction, selling for more than two million dollars. Overnight I was a multimillionaire. Then the movie rights sold. Big directors and big actors signed on. I was asked, or at least allowed, to co-write and co-produce the movie's screenplay. Truly, my life changed overnight.

"Some of you are here, presumably, because you want to be me. Or, at least, to be *like* me. You want to experience the Limousine Lifestyle of the Bestselling Author that my esteemed colleague Ms. McCullin talked about earlier from this very stage.

"I realize that, to a hopeful author, I am the dream. I know this. Five years after I began writing, Scott Simon on National Public Radio asked me, 'What does it feel like to have the life that thousands of aspiring writers covet?' I replied, 'Blessed.' " Zeke nodded slowly. "*Blessed*, I said." Then his expression changed. "Blessed," he repeated more softly. "Just six months later I would have changed that word to *cursed*.

"My wife, Emma, the love of my life, was a very private person. Private and shy. Almost pathologically shy. She was that way when I met her, dated her, and married her. She was also sweet and loving and content with the simple life we had when I was a teacher. I suppose we were poorly paired in this regard because I was not content. I wanted more. And I went headlong after it.

"After things took off in my career, she was quite uncomfortable with the invasion of our privacy. I thought I could temper the differences in our personalities by appearing camera shy. No pictures of me were put on my books. I rarely did television appearances, and newspaper interviewers were required to display a picture of my latest book instead of me.

"Once *People* magazine wanted to do a photo spread of the Cowell family. I knew it was a privilege. My publisher had pushed hard for the publicity, but Emma was mortified. We considered alternate ways of making the shoot happen until the photographer insisted on coming to our home and taking pictures of Emma and me cooking together. If you haven't noticed, *People* is big on kitchen shots. That doomed the photo shoot. While every author on the planet was beg-ging for media attention, I did my best to shun it.

"But being mysterious only fueled the public's interest and curiosity. Book sales continued to grow. And, with each book, each movie, each multimillion-dollar advance, the quiet life Emma and I had together faded a little bit more. My love slowly became a stranger to me—part of a former life I sometimes barely recognized anymore.

"I was gone almost all the time, on tour or speaking. Even touring I still maintained some anonymity. Photographs were not allowed. I grew a beard and wore dark glasses indoors even before Bono made it cool. Yes, the pay was good." He shook his head. "Actually, it was obscene—thirty thousand to fifty thousand dollars for a forty-minute speech. That was more than my entire annual salary just a few years earlier.

"And as the books kept coming, the powers that be pressured me for more. Two a year. Then three. I learned to write in airplanes and airports and in private suites in luxury hotels in cities that I never really got to see. I simultaneously went every-where and nowhere.

"When I wasn't touring in the U.S., there was Europe, Canada, South America, then Asia. And with each flight I put more miles between Emma and me, figuratively as well as literally. It was ironic, I suppose. Emma was the love of my life. I wrote my first book and dedicated it to her because she was my inspiration." His eyes turned dark. "She inspired me right out of her life.

"I knew we were going the wrong way. But I kept telling her it was only going to be a little while longer." He scratched his head. "I was right. Just not the way I meant.

"I didn't know the full extent of her pain; she wasn't a complainer, but she did become more withdrawn. She once said to me, 'Things are different with us.' I said, 'Yes, they're better. We have a beautiful home, nice cars, nice vacations, everything we always wanted.' She looked at me sadly, then said, 'I already had everything I wanted.' Then she said, 'But now I've lost you.'

"I was in Chicago on a book tour when it occurred to me that a child might be the solution to our marital rift. We had planned to have children one day. Maybe, I reasoned, if we had a baby, Emma wouldn't feel so alone. Maybe she wouldn't be so sad. Two months later she got pregnant. And I was gone when she found out. I was gone when she had her first doctor appointment. I was gone when she learned it was going to be a little girl.

"For the most part, the pregnancy went well, nothing unusual. Then one time, this one time . . ." His voice cracked. "Emma was five months preg-nant. I was packing to leave for another event when she said to me, 'I need you to stay.' I can't explain it, but her voice was different this time. There was something unusual about the way she asked. I looked in her eyes and I saw someone reaching out for me. Someone desperate. Some-one I used to know.

"Something told me that it was a turning poin in our marriage. I knew I needed to stay. I knew the former me, the man who married her, would have stayed." His voice fell with shame. "But Emma was right. I wasn't that man anymore. And I didn't stay. There were ten thousand strangers in an auditorium in Dallas who had shelled out thirty-seven bucks apiece to see me. Strangers. I chose them over my love."

At this moment he paused and I could see him change with emotion. I could feel his pain. "I was still in Dallas when the phone call came. Emma had hemorrhaged in the night. She bled to death."

Someone behind me gasped. The entire audience was still. Many were weeping. Zeke took off his glasses and wiped his eyes.

"She bled to death because I wasn't there. I don't know if she somehow knew—if perhaps she had had a premonition—but whether she knew or not doesn't matter. She was hanging over a cliff and she cried out to me to save her, and I . . ." He paused. "I let her go. Somewhere along the line I had traded in my heart for a check and a temporary seat on a bestseller list."

People around me were sniffing and rubbing their eyes with tissues. I couldn't keep the tears from rolling down my face.

"Coming home to an empty house—there was no home anymore. Only then did I fully under-stand that *she* was my home.

"I disappeared. I drank to take the edge off my pain. Then I kept drinking to stop my heart.

But that wasn't working, so I tried to overdose on painkillers. My housecleaner found me unconscious and called 911. She saved my life." He paused and looked out over the audience. "Why did I stop writing? I stopped writing because I was a fraud. I had betrayed love, so I was no longer worthy to write about it."

I could hear Samantha's stilted breathing. It matched my own. Zeke took a deep breath.

"So, my dear aspiring writers, here's a nickel's worth of advice from a man who's reached the pinnacle of success and thrown himself off. You have this beautiful dream before you and some of you are waiting for it to happen for your life to begin. I'm not here to take away your dreams. We need dreams. But you're in the middle of life right now. Never trade what you love for what's behind curtain B. Never. I would give everything I have, everything I've experienced, to see my love sitting in the front row right now." He took a deep breath. "I would give anything to be you —anonymous and hopeful you." His voice cracked with emotion. "I would give anything to be a poor English teacher in Bethlehem, Pennsyl-vania."

He turned and walked away. For a moment all four hundred–plus of us sat in stunned silence. Then the audience burst into thunderous applause and a standing ovation. Zeke never returned to accept it.

Chapter
Thirty-one

*The times we most want to forget
are likely the ones we never will.*

Kimberly Rossi's Diary

When the house lights rose, I sat there, paralyzed with emotion. My face was streaked with tears. The people around me began to rise, moving out of the room slowly, as if in a daze. I just sat there wiping my eyes.

"Did you know any of that?" Samantha asked.

"I didn't know it was him."

"You need to talk to him."

Tears filled my eyes. "It's too late," I said. "I already ruined it. He'll just think I want H. T. Cowell." I breathed out slowly. "It's time for me to go home."

With the crowds milling about it took us nearly half an hour to get a taxi. Samantha's flight was thirty minutes before mine, and I was a little nervous that she might miss it, but she wasn't. "Stop worrying about other people's worries," she said. "You have enough of your own. Besides, I've slept in airports before. It's no big deal."

"I'm going to miss you," I said.

"No you're not," she said. She kissed my cheek. "We're going to keep in touch."

We got to the airport with a few minutes to spare. Samantha was on a different airline and we stopped at her terminal first. I got out with her.

"I'm so glad I met you," she said.

"Me too. You saved me."

"No, you saved me. You have my number. You need to come see me in Montana. I'll take you horseback riding after the snow's gone."

"Next summer," I said.

"Next summer is perfect," she said. "I'm holding you to it." We hugged. As we embraced she whispered into my ear, "I'm sorry things didn't work out with Zeke. But you wouldn't trade it, would you? I mean, how many people get to break H. T. Cowell's heart?"

I smiled sadly. "Just two of us, I guess."

"You watch, you'll probably end up in one of his books. I can see it now: *The Mistletoe Inn*."

"I hope not."

"And I hope so." She kissed me, then reached down and grabbed her bag. "Next summer," she said. "Au revoir."

"Good-bye," I said. She turned and walked into the terminal. I got back into the taxi. "Delta, please."

"Headed home?" the driver asked.

"Yes."

"Just in time for Christmas. Did you have a good stay in Vermont?"

"I don't know," I said.

The driver said nothing.

Chapter
Thirty-two

*We cannot run fast enough
to escape some failures.*

Kimberly Rossi's Diary

On the flight back to Denver my mind kept changing channels. *If only I had known the whole story,* I thought. But that's the point of love, isn't it? We never know the whole story. The true test of our hearts is how we respond with what we have. Zeke had put himself out there, and I had rejected him. I had failed miserably. I had failed him. He was a beautiful soul, more than I deserved. I hoped he was okay, then I thought, *Don't flatter yourself. He's H. T. Cowell. I'm sure there are already a thousand women lined up for the chance you just blew. Especially after his real love story hits the press. It's better than any of the love stories he's ever written.*

The flight home was direct and, with the time change, I landed just before sunset at around 5 p.m. In my absence the city had been hit by several large snowstorms and from the air Denver looked like a ruffled, white linen sheet.

I picked up my bag and took the shuttle out to my car, which wasn't easy to find since it looked like an igloo covered with more than a foot of snow. I got my snow brush from the backseat, dug out my car, then drove home to Thornton.

My apartment was as dark and cold as I felt inside. I had forgotten how quiet it was. I switched on the lights, turned up the heat, undressed, and took a warm shower. A half hour later, as my water heater began to run out of hot water, I got out and dressed, then went to make myself some dinner. My refrigerator was pretty much bare, so I made some ramen noodles, then drove to the grocery store to pick up some food.

As the cashier rang up the woman in front of me, I examined her purchases. Along with her groceries she had a mass-market paperback romance, the kind usually referred to as a "bodice ripper," with a long-haired, bare-chested hunk on the cover.

"We don't sell as many of those as we used to," the checker said to the woman. "These days, people just download them from the Internet."

"I'm old-fashioned," the woman said. "I still like the feel of paper. And I like to read in the bath. I'd probably just drop an e-book in the water."

"I know what you mean. If I really like an author, sometimes I'll buy the e-book and the paper book." She finished ringing the woman up. "That'll be forty-nine-oh-five. You can scan your card right there."

As the woman ran her credit card through the reader, the cashier said, "I heard on the news that H. T. Cowell is coming out with another book."

The woman looked up with interest. "I thought he was dead."

"No. He just stopped writing for a while. But he's come out of retirement."

"I loved his books," she said.

"Don't we all? I've already ordered it online."

"Thanks for the tip."

"No problem. Have a good day." The cashier turned to me. "Evening, darling. Paper or plastic?"

"Plastic, please."

She began ringing up my items. "That's a good deal on those red peppers. Do you have a customer discount card?"

"Yes. Right here." I handed her my card.

She scanned it, then handed it back. "That will save you a little."

As she bagged my purchases, I said, "I overheard some of your conversation. I've met H. T. Cowell."

"Is that right? What was he like?"

Unexpectedly my eyes filled up with tears. "He was . . ." A tear fell down my cheek. I suddenly wished I hadn't said anything. "Sorry," I said, wiping my eyes with my sleeve.

The woman smiled a little. "I used to get the same way whenever I'd read one of his books. The man makes women cry for a living." She finished ringing up my groceries. "Have a good evening."

"You too."

As I walked to my car I realized that I would never be able to escape him.

Chapter
Thirty-three

*Routine is the refuge of cowards,
failures, and the wise.*

Kimberly Rossi's Diary

I was glad to be back at work on Monday morning. I needed something to get my mind off my pain. I had only been in my office for ten minutes before Steve came in.

"I'm so glad you're back. Rachelle's so distracted with her upcoming nuptials that she keeps making mistakes. How was your book conference?"

"It was a writers' conference," I said. "It was good."

"Good," he echoed. "Well, if you hit it big with your book, that doesn't mean you can just leave us all behind."

"I wouldn't be looking for my replacement anytime soon."

His smile fell. "I shouldn't be sorry to hear that, but I am. You deserve a break."

"Thanks, Steve."

"Welcome home," he said.

The day was busy. Car sales are always big right before Christmas. Our clientele were the kind of people who would call on Christmas Eve and say, "I want a new car for my husband delivered on Christmas Eve with a ribbon on it" and we'd move heaven and earth to make it happen. All morning long I had a steady flow of clients in my office. I finally got a short lunch break at one.

As I walked into the break room, Rachelle was eating lunch with Charlene, one of our newer salespeople. Rachelle looked up at me as I entered. "Hey, Kim, didn't you just meet H. T. Cowell at some conference?"

Now Zeke has followed me to work. I nodded. "Yeah. He was the keynote speaker." I walked over and took a can of Diet Coke from the refrigerator.

"That's so cool," Rachelle said. "There was an article about him in *USA Today* this morning. And you know how no one knows what he looks like? There was almost a full-page picture of him. He's gorgeous."

"What did the article say?" I asked.

"It said he's coming out with a new book and the movie rights have already been sold. And he finally told why he stopped writing. It was because his wife died. I mean, is that romantic or what? After all his success, she committed suicide."

"Why would she do that?" Charlene said. "People die for that kind of life, not because they got it."

"She didn't kill herself," I said. "It was an accident."

Rachelle shook her head. "No, she killed herself. I just read it in the paper."

"Then whoever wrote the article got it wrong," I said. "His wife was pregnant and died of a hemorrhage. It was an accident."

Rachelle didn't back down. "And you know this because . . . ?"

"Because he told me," I snapped. The sound of my voice fairly echoed, leaving me embarrassed. The two women just looked at me.

"H. T. Cowell told you how his wife died?" Rachelle said.

"You talked to H. T. Cowell?" Charlene asked.

"Yes."

Rachelle looked at me skeptically. "You mean, like, not in a crowd, but one-on-one."

I felt like I was talking to six-year-olds. Obnoxious six-year-olds. "Yes, I talked to him like we're talking now."

Rachelle looked like it was all she could do not to laugh. "So you and H. T. Cowell are now BFFs."

"I didn't say that."

"But you're talking about really personal things . . ."

I breathed out slowly to relieve my annoyance with her. "Yes. We went on a few dates."

Rachelle looked so incredulous I thought she was going to burst out laughing. "You dated H. T. Cowell?" she said.

"Yes, I dated H. T. Cowell. Why is that so hard to believe?"

The two women just grinned like they were sharing an inside joke.

"I don't know," Rachelle said. "Why wouldn't we believe that you're secretly dating one of the most famous writers in the world?"

Both women continued to gape at me. After a moment I said, "You're right. I wouldn't believe it either. Why would he date someone like me?"

I took my drink back to my office, shut my door, and cried.

Chapter
Thirty-four

*I'm not sure where home is anymore,
but I want to be there.*

Kimberly Rossi's Diary

My father called that night on the way home from work. "You didn't call."

"Sorry. I wasn't feeling well last night. How are you feeling?"

"I'm fine," he said dismissively. "How was the rest of the retreat?"

"It was fine."

"For as much as it cost, I expected more than *fine*."

"Sorry, it was great. It was much better than the San Francisco one."

"How was Cowell? Was he worth the money?"

I hesitated. "I'd rather not talk about it."

"So the conference was good, but Cowell was a disappointment."

"I didn't say that. It's just . . ." There was a long pause. "It's just complicated."

I'm sure my father knew that there was more; he could read me like a Times Square billboard, but he also knew when not to press. "You're still coming out for Christmas, aren't you?"

"Yes. I'll be there Sunday night if that's okay."

"Of course."

"I'd come sooner if I could, but work's crazy and I was gone all last week."

"I understand."

I sighed. "I've got to get out of here."

"Maybe it's time you moved back, girl."

For the first time ever I didn't launch into a defense. After a moment I said, "Maybe it is."

To my surprise my father didn't jump on my concession. Either he was too surprised or he heard the defeat in my voice. Probably the latter. He finally said, "I'm just glad you're coming when you can. You're Christmas to me."

"Thank you, Dad. I'll see you Sunday night."

As I hung up the phone I pushed out the thought that this might be the last Christmas we'd ever have together.

Chapter
Thirty-five

Finally, good news. Finally.

Kimberly Rossi's Diary

The Las Vegas casinos do a large advertising push outside the United States during the holidays, so the airport is always crowded around Christmas with international tourists. My plane landed at nine-thirty, and after fighting the crowds for almost an hour, I retrieved my bag and met my father at the curb.

As usual he got out of his car to greet me. I was stunned when I saw him. As thin as he already was at Thanksgiving, he'd probably lost another ten or more pounds. Also, his eyes looked hollow and ringed as if he hadn't slept well for a while. It took effort not to show my concern. In spite of his condition his face beamed with joy. "How was your flight, sweetie?"

"You know, the usual holiday insanity."

As he put his arms around me I could feel how different his body was. The cancer was taking its toll. I still couldn't believe that they were making him wait until February to operate. It was obvious to me that at the rate he was deteriorating, February might be too late.

"It's so good to see you," he said, kissing my cheek. He opened my door and took my bag and set it in the backseat. I sadly noticed that he had a little trouble lifting my bag. He'd lost muscle as well.

As we were driving away from the airport he turned off the radio, then said to me, "I have some good news."

I looked over at him. "You're getting married."

"I said *good* news."

"Tell me."

"I have a new oncologist."

"At the VA?"

He smiled, excited to answer. "No, at the Henderson Clinic. And they're going to operate this coming Friday."

My heart leapt. "What?"

"It gets better. The doctor's name is Lance Bangerter. He's ranked as one of the top-five colon cancer experts in the country."

Even though my father was merging onto the freeway I leaned over and hugged him. "Thank you, thank you, thank you!" My eyes welled up. "You have no idea how much this means to me."

"I think I do," he replied. "And thank God. He's the one who arranged it."

"I thought your insurance didn't cover the institute."

"It doesn't," he said.

"I don't care," I said. "Whatever it takes. I'll give you every penny I have."

He looked at me lovingly. "I know you would, sweetheart. But you don't have to. Things have worked out. Fate has smiled on me."

"It couldn't smile on a more deserving man."

"I don't know about that," he said. "But the longer I live the more certain I am that God is in the details."

We pulled into the driveway. My father wouldn't let me carry in my bag, and even though it pained me to see him struggle with my suitcase, I knew it would be demoralizing to him if I didn't let him take it. As we walked into the house I noticed the fish tank was gone.

"Where are your fish?"

"They died," he said, shaking his head. "So I sold everything. I guess I chose the wrong hobby."

I looked around the house. As usual, my father had put up his Christmas tree in the front room to the side of the television. It was one of those expensive fake PVC ones that looked real. It had red and silver baubles and strings of flashing colored lights and a lit star on top. There were presents under the tree, which I knew were for me. I was dismayed that in addition to the conference he'd bought me more gifts.

"Those had better not be for me," I said.

"Who else would they be for?" he said.

"You already gave me the writers' retreat."

"Let an old man have his fun."

"You're not old," I said. Then I smiled. "But you are fun."

After we were in my room, my father said, "I guess I'll turn in. I'm sure you're exhausted; it's almost midnight in Denver."

I knew that he was much more tired than I was, but I said, "Good night, Dad. I'll see you in the morning."

As he started out of my room I said, "Dad."

He turned back.

"Thank you for changing your mind about that clinic."

He smiled. "Remember, sweetheart. Our best years are still to come."

After he left I undressed, turned out the light, and climbed under the covers. As I lay in bed I actually smiled. Things hadn't been going my way lately, but now the most important thing had. My father was getting the care he needed. I didn't know how we'd pay for the treatment, but at the moment, I didn't care. All that mattered was that he had a chance. I knew that in spite of all my pain I was still a very lucky woman. It made me sad that I wanted to call Zeke and tell him.

Chapter
Thirty-six

*Change is coming. I don't know how
I know this, but I can feel it.*

Kimberly Rossi's Diary

I got up early Christmas Eve morning, put on my sweats, and went for a walk. The temperature was in the high sixties, again a veritable heat wave compared to Denver. *Why do I live in Denver?*

There was already heavy traffic on the main roads, and I guessed that the procrastinators were out in force frantically pursuing those last-minute Christmas purchases.

Looking out over the horizon I breathed in the luxurious dry desert air. It was time for a change in my life. A new year was coming. A new year, a new life. Denver is a nice city but Las Vegas was home. I was finally ready to come home. I needed to be home. My father would need help through his recovery. I owed him that. More than that, I wanted to help him. He was the one person who had never let me down. It was about time I returned the favor.

The more I thought about moving back the more it made sense. There were dozens of car dealerships in Las Vegas and at least three Lexus dealerships. With my experience and references I wouldn't have trouble finding a job. I would miss Steve. But not anyone else. Not Rachelle. Definitely not Rachelle.

The idea of moving home filled me with joy.

I wasn't scheduled to be back at work until January 2. That gave me the entire week after Christmas to find employment and get things in order. I just needed to make it through Christmas.

Chapter
Thirty-seven

*For individuals, as for nations,
there are days that live in infamy.*

Kimberly Rossi's Diary

The power of Christmas is its capacity to evoke memories. For most, the familiar songs and decorations bring back cherished feelings of Christmas past—fond memories of shared experiences with family and loved ones.

For my father and me, that power was turned against us and Christmas brought out the worst of memories. Crippling memories. Christmas Day 1995 was the day we found my mother dead.

For me 1995 carried its own special horror. It was still morning. I had opened my presents with my father, as my mother was in bed with a migraine.

I still remember what I got that year. Trauma has a way of indelibly linking the incidentals to the profound. I received boxes of Swedish Fish and Lemonheads, some clothes, the album *Pieces of You* by Jewel, and my big present, a Sony Discman CD player.

I had just opened the last of my gifts when my father got up to check on my mother. It seemed that he was gone a long time and I put on my earphones and started listening to "Who Will Save Your Soul" on my new CD player. Even with the music playing I heard him cry out. I ran into the bedroom to find my father on his knees bent over my mother's still body. He was sobbing.

Chapter
Thirty-eight

*The truth will set us free
not only from external shackles but,
more often than not, our own.*

Kimberly Rossi's Diary

When I got back to the house, my father was in the kitchen making breakfast. Christmas music was playing.

"Good morning," he said.

"What are we doing today?" I asked.

"We've got cooking to do," he said. "And, of course, dinner at the Jade Dragon."

"Of course," I said. Every Christmas Eve, except during the years I was married to Marcus, my father and I had gone out to dinner for Chinese at the Jade Dragon Restaurant, a Christmas Eve tradition we'd loosely borrowed from our perennial Christmas favorite, *A Christmas Story*—the movie with Ralphie and his Red Ryder BB gun. "I have a little shopping to do."

"Just take the car," he said.

I had already purchased my father's Christmas presents; I just wanted to get out, hoping to keep ahead of my panic attacks. I also wanted to scout out some car dealerships. They were open, of course, and there were people inside. As I said, there are always those last-minute Christmas purchases.

If I was trying to outrun my anxiety, I was failing. You can't outrun fog. As the evening fell my anxiety grew worse. My father recognized it, of course. I'm sure he was expecting it. We went to dinner at six. My father told jokes and funny stories about the VA, but I just grew more somber. We finished our meal and drove home, my father growing increasingly uncomfortable with my moodiness.

As we walked into the house he asked, "What's wrong?"

"You know what's wrong," I said. "I hate Christmas."

"I know," he said. "You always have. At least since . . ."

"Since my mother annihilated it?" I said, saying what he wouldn't.

He paused, and for a moment there was just silence. Then my father said, "Honey, I need to tell you something about your mother."

"I don't want to talk about her."

"I know. And for years I've honored your feelings. But this time, you're going to listen to me. Let's go in the family room."

I was stunned by the gravity of his voice. My father had never before spoken to me this way about my mother. I followed him into the family room and sat down on the couch across from his chair. He took a deep breath and looked at me with a somber expression.

"Kim, it wasn't easy raising you alone, especially after all you went through. But I did my best. I'm sorry I wasn't a better father."

I looked at him incredulously. "Don't say that. You're the best father I could ever have."

"I don't know," he said. "I've always believed in letting you be you and make your own decisions. But sometimes I think that might have been a mistake. There've been times in my life when I've remained silent when I should have spoken up. Like when you married Marcus. I knew he was rotten. I should have told you no. I don't know if you would have listened to me, but I regret not doing more to stop that.

"But there's one thing that I feel even worse about than Marcus and that's your mother. There's something you need to know about her—something that I don't think you fully understand—and you need to understand. You need to listen to me carefully." He leaned forward, and even though he looked old and tired, his eyes were strong and clear. "Kim, you need to know that I not only loved your mother, I still do. And knowing what I know now, I would marry her all over again."

I couldn't believe what he was saying. "Why?"

"I knew your mother at her best. You don't know that side of her, but she was sunshine. She was my one true love. She healed me from the pain of war. She was there in my hardest times. She was there in my nightmares.

"When you were little, you thought your

mother's name was Tessa. That's because you heard me call her by my nickname for her, Tesoro. That's Italian for *treasure*. That's what she was to me. My treasure.

"The first years of our marriage were beautiful. She struggled a little with depression, it ran in her family, but she fought it and she always came back.

"It wasn't until after she gave birth to you that she went into the deepest depression I had ever seen in her. It was something chemical. She fought it for years. She did everything every doctor, every counselor, told her to do.

"One time, at a holistic counselor's advice, she went off all of her medications cold turkey. I sat with her through the night as she went through withdrawal. She sweated out her clothing and shook and wept, but she didn't give up. She did whatever she thought she had to do. Not for herself, but for you and me. But it didn't get better; it got worse. It began to overcome her.

"Depression is a horrible thing. It overtakes a person like a parasite, feeding off their hope and self-esteem until there's nothing left. Mom wasn't trying to run away from you or me, she was trying to run away from the monster that was eating her from the inside out.

"What happened when she took her life was unimaginably painful for you. And for me. But you need to know how hard she fought to be with us. In the end, she lost the battle, but she fought as courageously as anyone I've ever seen." He looked into my eyes. "Now answer me honestly. If cancer overtook me now, would you think that I had abandoned you?"

I began to cry. "Of course not."

"No. You wouldn't. And you shouldn't with your mother. People make judgments about suicide and depression based on their own experience, but that's like me describing the surface of Mars. I've never been there. I can only guess what it's like.

"Depression alters the mind's ability to think rationally. Things that would horrify someone in their right mind suddenly seem like a good idea. Like ending their life. They might even believe that they're doing the right thing for those they love." A tear fell down my father's cheek. "Before her death, she left a letter. In it, she said that she had finally set me and you free to be happy. She thought it was the right thing."

I was quiet for a moment, then said softly, "You want me to forgive her?"

To my surprise he shook his head. "Forgiving her won't help her. She's gone. What I want is for you to forgive yourself."

"Forgive myself for what?"

"One thing I know is that somewhere deep inside, in spite of what we tell ourselves, part of all survivors believe that they could have changed the outcome by doing something different.

"Then we try to ease our pain with anger. But anger isn't strength. It only masks itself as strength. It's weakness. At its core, it's fear. Fear of facing what might be the truth."

I bowed my head. My mind felt as if it were spinning.

"I should have talked to you about this much, much sooner. But for so many years I didn't understand all this myself. I was struggling with my own paradox. You see, Mom's depression changed after she gave birth to you. If she had never given birth . . ."

I looked up. "You're saying it's my fault?"

"Absolutely not," he said firmly. "You had no say in the matter. But I did. And I've wondered so many times . . ." He looked down. When he looked back up there were tears in his eyes. "She knew. In her last letter, she wrote, 'I would do it again for my Kimberly. She is the one beautiful light to shine from my darkness. Even if I cannot be the mother I want to be, the mother she deserves, I have never regretted my decision to have her.' "

My father began to openly cry. Then, at that moment, a dam of emotion broke, flooding through my entire being. I began sobbing. My father came over and put his arms around me as my body heaved.

It took me a while to realize what was happening. After all these years I was finally mourning my mother.

My father held me for a long while. After I finally began to calm, he said, "Let's go to bed." He helped me up and went into the bathroom. He came out holding a warm, wet washcloth, which he handed to me.

"You've been through something traumatic tonight. I want you to not think about it anymore but put this on your face and relax. Your mind needs to rest. An army psychiatrist told me that helps."

"Thank you," I said.

"Kim," he said. "Remember, our best years are ahead of us."

We hugged and I went to my room. I turned out the lights, lay back in bed, and put the hot cloth on my face. I did my best to clear my mind. For the first Christmas Eve in years I felt peace. "Merry Christmas," I said to myself. "And a happy New Year." I quickly fell asleep.

Chapter
Thirty-nine

Nothing done with joy is done in vain.

Kimberly Rossi's Diary

My father woke me the next morning with his Bible in hand and a cheerful "Merry Christmas." It had always been our tradition to read from the second chapter of Luke on Christmas morning. Afterward we went out to the tree and opened presents. I had bought him a big bag of turkey jerky, socks, a plush bathrobe, and a book on raising saltwater fish. "You can take that back," I said.

He had bought me a new laptop computer. "This is too much," I said.

"It's for your writing," he said. "And here." He handed me another present to unwrap. Inside was a describer's dictionary. "I read online that that really helps."

I didn't know what to say. "Dad, no one's going to publish me."

"Who cares?" he said. "I'm not going to get signed by a record label but it doesn't stop me from singing in the shower."

"It should," I said, laughing.

He also laughed. "It should, but it won't. So you write because you love to write. It's how you sing. Remember that."

I couldn't help but smile. "Thanks, Dad."

After we opened our presents we had our traditional Christmas morning breakfast of crepes with apricot jam and whipped cream. My father made the world's best crepes.

"It was a profound night last night," he said as we ate. "How'd you sleep?"

"I slept really well. The best I have in years." I smiled. "At least until I woke with a cold, wet washcloth on my face."

He smiled.

I took another bite of crepe, then said, "I've been doing a lot of thinking. And I think it's time for some change in my life. So I've made a decision. I'm moving back home." I looked into his eyes. "If that's okay."

A smile spread across his face. "That's wonderful."

"That way I can be here if you need any help and just be with you. I miss it here."

"That makes me so happy," he said. "That's the best Christmas present ever."

"Good. So I'll start looking for a job tomorrow." I ate a little more, then I said, "You know, it's strange, but I have a feeling that you're right. Maybe our best years are still to come."

My father, who hadn't stopped smiling since my announcement, said, "Oh, they are, honey. More than you know. Now hurry up and eat. We've got cooking to do."

• • •

As we got ready for Christmas dinner I noticed that my father had placed an extra setting at the table. "Will Chuck or Joel be joining us?" I asked.

He shook his head. "No. I'm sorry, I didn't tell you, Chuck passed away."

I stopped washing the potatoes. "When?"

"While you were at the conference. I was with him when he went. I'm grateful for that. No one should die alone."

"How's Joel doing?" I asked. "I was thinking of looking him up while I was here."

"That might not be a good idea," my father said.

"Why is that?"

"His wife came back."

"Really?" I said. "That's a surprise."

"It was for Joel too. He called me two weeks ago and told me that she came to see him. She asked him if he would forgive her and take her back."

"And he took her back?"

"Oh yes. Sometimes, when you least expect it, people do the right thing. And the best news, they're going to start trying to have children."

"He can do that? I mean, physically . . . ?"

"No. They'll have to use insemination. But that's not what makes a man a father."

"Then Alice is coming?"

"No," he said. "Prying her away from her grandchildren will take a lot stronger man than I am."

"Her loss," I said.

"She's perfectly happy with the situation. Something about grandchildren is magical. I hope to discover that myself someday."

"Pressure," I said. "Then who's coming?"

"Just a business associate of mine. I've been helping him with a project. He lives back east and was here alone on business, so I invited him over. He'll be here in a few minutes."

"What kind of project?" I asked.

"Nothing too exciting. Personnel stuff. He ran into one of my old employees from Maverick. She told him about me and he was looking for someone in Vegas.

"But here's the remarkable part—he's friends with Dr. Bangerter. He's the one who arranged for him to see me. In fact, he has so much clout, Dr. Bangerter actually came to the house to meet with me."

"One of the top oncologists in the country made a house call?"

"I know, you could have knocked me over with a feather. I guess it helps to have the right friends."

"I'm so happy, Dad."

As I went back to the potatoes, the doorbell rang.

"Unless you're expecting someone," my father said, "that's probably our guest. Would you mind getting the door?"

"Sure." I started walking toward the foyer. "What's his name?"

"You'll know," he said.

"Why would I know?"

"Just trust me."

I opened the door. Zeke was standing on our front porch.

Chapter
Forty

A new song has begun.

Kimberly Rossi's Diary

I just stood there. The moment was like something out of a dream and I was frozen in it, unsure of what to do next.

Zeke smiled. "I take it your father didn't tell you I was coming."

"No."

My father walked up behind me. "Kim, show some manners. Invite Zeke in."

"Sorry," I said, still in shock. I stepped back as Zeke walked into our house. My father and Zeke shook hands.

"How are you, Rob?" Zeke asked.

"Well, thank you. And very grateful. Dr. Bangerter has been very helpful. Thank you for making this possible."

"It's my pleasure," he said.

I stood there, my eyes darting back and forth between the two of them. "How do you know each other?"

"He called," my father said, as if it were just the most natural thing in the world. "He asked for my permission to date my daughter and I said yes. You know, he's the first man you've dated who had the class to call me." He turned back to Zeke. "We're still getting ready to eat. I'll give you two a moment to catch up."

"Thank you," Zeke said.

As my father walked out of the room Zeke turned back to me. "Merry Christmas," he said.

I was still in shock. "Thank you for helping my father."

"I can see why you idolize him. He's a good man."

I stood there still unsure of what to say.

"I'm guessing that you were surprised to learn that Zeke Faulkner and H. T. Cowell are the same man."

"Why didn't you tell me you were H. T. Cowell?"

"You never asked."

"That's not something I usually go around asking people."

He grinned. "That's understandable."

"Why did you say your name was Zeke?"

"I've gone by Zeke my whole life. H. T. stands for Hezekiah Tobias," he said. "Hezekiah. Who names a child Hezekiah? Tell me you wouldn't go by Zeke too."

In spite of my emotion I almost smiled. "Why did you go to the writers' conference?"

"I was invited to speak," he said. "My publisher decided that it would be the perfect timing for my 'coming out,' which is why there was so much national press. But I went to the conference early to be with the unpublished writers. That was for me. I wanted to feel their passion. I wanted to remember why it was I started writing to begin with. If I had told them who I was they would have acted different."

He was right about that. I wouldn't have been able to talk to him.

"I wanted to talk to you after your speech," I said. "But I didn't know what to say after behaving so badly. Twice." I looked into his eyes. "I didn't think you would want to see me."

He looked at me for a moment, then said, "I told you in New York that I had fallen in love with you. I had. After the retreat I couldn't get you off my mind. I wasn't going to give up on love. I did that once before. I wasn't going to do it again."

"How did you find us?"

"That part was easy. You told me that your father had paid for the retreat, so I called the organizers and asked for his contact information. I called your father and introduced myself. I told him that you and I had met at the conference and that I would like his permission to court his daughter and that my intentions were honorable."

"Honorable," I repeated. "He must have loved that."

Zeke smiled. "He seemed impressed. But trust me, he wasn't easy on me. So I thought it best that I flew out to meet him. I told him that we had had a difficult parting and I asked his advice on how best to approach you. He thought that the best time for me to see you would be now. So I made arrangements to return."

"And the doctor?"

"I knew how upset you were about the treatment your father was receiving. I've raised millions of dollars for the Henderson Institute, and Dr. Bangerter once said that if he could ever do anything for me to just ask. So I asked. It was a token of my appreciation to your father for his help. And maybe a little bribe."

"A bribe?"

"It's the law of reciprocity. I knew that if I made some magnanimous gesture you would at least have to give me a chance to win back your love."

"You never lost it," I said.

For a moment we looked at each other, then we kissed.

After several minutes of kissing, Zeke leaned back and said excitedly, "I have a Christmas present for you." He took an envelope from his jacket and handed it to me.

"What is it?"

"Open it."

Inside the envelope was a letter from Trish Todd, an editor at the Simon & Schuster Adult Publishing Group. "What's this?"

"I took your book to my editor and she liked it. The letter says if you're willing to make a few revisions, which I would be happy to help you with, they would like to offer you a contract."

I was speechless. I looked up from the letter. "You mean they're really going to publish my book?"

He smiled. "Yes they are. I also let them know that I would be helping to promote your book with my readers. If I still have any."

"The whole world is waiting for your next book," I said. "Everyone is talking about it." After looking at him for a moment, I said, "Why are you being so good to me?"

He looked at me intensely, then said, "I thought you might ask that. And I am prepared with three answers. First, I'm a romance writer. I love happy endings. Second, because you are immensely loveable. And third, most of all, I heard the music and I wanted to dance with you."

I looked at him for a moment, then said, "And when the music stops?"

A broad smile slowly crossed his face and he again took me in his arms and we kissed. When we finally parted he said, "When, and if, the music ever stops there's no need to worry."

"Why not?"

"Because when the music stops, that's when we make our own."

epilogue

Zeke stayed with me the week after Christmas. I never went looking for a job; Zeke kept me too busy working on my book. Imagine being tutored by one of the world's greatest authors. He taught me how to be vulnerable in print. He taught me to love my readers. He taught me how to write with honesty.

It was an amazing experience to see how he coaxed words from thin air—like a magician. It seemed to me that his process was more like discovering a book than creating it. William Faulkner once said, "If I had not existed, someone else would have written me, Hemingway, Dostoyevsky, all of us." Zeke believed that. He taught me to believe that as well.

My life is new. On New Year's Eve I went alone to my mother's grave and took her a flower. An anthurium. Somewhere in a recently unlocked room of my mind I remembered that she loved anthuriums. I knelt down and kissed her stone and apologized to her. I thanked her for giving me life at the expense of her own. For the first time in my life I saw her not as a traitor or a failure but as a real person just doing her best. For the first time since I was a child I loved her again. And, not coincidentally, I felt her love.

I tried to get my father to join Zeke and me for dinner that night at a fancy restaurant at the Bellagio. He wouldn't budge. "I'm too old for all that New Year's hoopla," he said. "I just want to go to bed." Later I learned why he had refused. At 12:01 on January 1, 2013, Zeke asked me to marry him. My father was awake when we got home. This time he was happy with my choice.

The ring Zeke had given me that night was on loan from a jewelry store as he wanted to pick out our rings together. (It had a diamond that would have made Catherine McCullin salivate.) The next day we went ring shopping at Tiffany, and as we looked at settings fit for a princess I realized what I really wanted. That evening I asked my father if I could have my mother's tiny half-carat rose-gold engagement ring. Nothing could have made my father happier. It made Zeke happy too.

After our engagement Zeke went back with me to Denver to help move me out of my apartment. He also went with me to the dealership to get my things. I think he especially wanted to go after I told him the story of how Rachelle and Charlene had mocked me when I told them that I had dated H. T. Cowell. As I introduced Zeke to Rachelle and Charlene, he referred to himself as H. T. Cowell. It was the only time I've ever heard him do that. You should have seen their faces. We laughed about it all through dinner.

Zeke had no problem with the idea of moving to Las Vegas, especially while my father was dealing with his cancer. He said that he had always wanted to live in the West. At first I thought he was just being kind, but I learned otherwise. He secretly wanted to be a cowboy, which he ended up writing a book about. (What woman doesn't love a cow-boy?) That summer he went with me to Montana to see Samantha and ride horses. He bought a ranch.

My father's surgery and post treatment were successful. Today he is three years in remission. We bought a home just ten minutes away from his. He's still volunteering at the VA, but he's also spending more time with Alice, who it turns out is a rabid H. T. Cowell fan. It's kind of annoying.

As you probably remember, Zeke's return to writing rocked the publishing world, and I traveled all around the world with him on a book tour. London, Paris, Tokyo, Sydney, and Warsaw. He arranged the release of his third book to coincide with the release of mine, *The Mistletoe Promise*. Not surprisingly, both of our books hit the *New York Times* bestseller list—though of course his was number one and mine was eight. Still, I'm now a *New York Times* bestselling author. When we got the advance copy of the bestseller list I think Zeke was happier for me than for himself. Actually, I know he was. Yes, I know I hit the list because of his help—both with his help writing and his legion of fans—but it still feels wonderful. I feel like I've done something that matters. I actually get fan mail.

On May 3, 2014, Zeke and I were married in San Gimignano, Italy, the birthplace of my father's parents. Samantha was my maid of honor. She brought her new husband, Walter. He's a great guy. For the record, I don't think she settled. I'm now thinking of writing a love story that takes place in Italy, and I keep wishing that I had gone to that session at the Mistletoe Inn Writers' Conference. You know the one—*Putting the Rome Back in Romance*. Our wedding made all the magazines, which was much better than the last time I got press.

Speaking of which, two months after our wedding I got a call from Marcus. He knew about Zeke and my writing. He wanted to know if I would write a reference letter for him for a high school teaching position. I almost agreed until I thought about those young girls he would be around and declined.

The most important thing Zeke has taught me about love has nothing to do with books Romance novels are all about desire and happily-ever-after, but happily-ever-after doesn't come from desire—at least not the kind portrayed in pulp romances. Real love is not to desire a person but to desire their happiness—sometimes even at the expense of our own happiness. Real love is to expand our own capacity for tolerance and caring, to actively seek another's well-being. All else is simply a charade of self-interest.

Zeke taught me that. Not through words but by example. He's taught me how to dance. And we're getting good at making our own music.

My father was right all along. The best years of our lives are ahead of us.

About the Author

Richard Paul Evans is the #1 bestselling author of *The Christmas Box*. Each of his more than thirty novels has been a *New York Times* bestseller. There are more than 20 million copies of his books in print worldwide, translated into more than twenty-four languages. He is the recipient of numerous awards, including the American Mothers Book Award, the *Romantic Times* Best Women's Novel of the Year Award, the German Audience Gold Award for Romance, four Religion Communicators Council Wilbur Awards, *The Washington Times* Humanitarian of the Century Award, and the Volunteers of America National Empathy Award. He lives in Salt Lake City, Utah, with his wife, Keri, and their five children. You can learn more about Richard on Facebook at:

www.facebook.com/RPEfans,
or visit his website
(and read his weekly blog) at
www.richardpaulevans.com.

Center Point Large Print
600 Brooks Road / PO Box 1
Thorndike, ME 04986-0001 USA

(207) 568-3717

US & Canada:
1 800 929-9108
www.centerpointlargeprint.com